POLO
SOLO
JERRY KENNEALY

D0003821

ST. MARTIN'S PRESS/NEW YORK

POLO SOLO

Copyright © 1987 by Jerry Kennealy

All rights reserved. No part of this book may be used or reproduced in any manner whatsoever without written permission except in the case of brief quotations embodied in critical articles or reviews. For information address St. Martin's Press, 175 Fifth Avenue, New York, N.Y. 10010.

Library of Congress Catalog Card Number: 87-1693

ISBN: 0-312-91074-6   Can. ISBN: 0-312-91075-4

Printed in the United States of America

First St. Martin's Press mass market edition/February 1988

10 9 8 7 6 5 4 3 2 1

A SHOT IN THE DARK

"Don't ever touch me like that again, Polo."

"Oh, you don't like being touched? How do you think she felt, Jimmy? You set her up first, didn't you?"

He reached back with his right hand before throwing the punch, which gave me plenty of time to step inside and block it with my left arm. I ground my heels into the carpet and swiveled in, throwing my right elbow into his stomach. The elbow is a wonderful thing. Nice to have for leaning on bars, or flicking on the light switch when your hands are full. But when you use it as a weapon, it can do a lot of damage. It's small, hard, relatively pointed at the end. The tip of my elbow punctured Kostas' stomach muscles, and his breath whooshed out like air from a punctured tire. I backed away and let him slowly sink to his knees. I slapped a twenty on the bar. "Fix Mr. Kostas and his friends a drink. I think they'll need it."

Not too shabby for an exit line, huh?

For my wife, Shirley

1

The two men watched the TV screen intently.

The mayor of San Francisco took off her oversized sunglasses and smiled uncertainly. She was wearing a pair of pink running shorts, pink Adidases, and a matching pink tank top. A woven multicolored band held her tawny-colored hair back from her face. It was the same outfit she'd worn when *Time* magazine had her on its cover, jogging across the Golden Gate Bridge, the caption asking, "RUNNING FOR HIGHER OFFICE?"

On the screen a man approached her. He was tall, dark-haired, and very young. He grabbed her hand and led her to a bed, the cover down, the sheets rumpled. As he started helping her out of her tank top, they were joined by a girl, not more than a year or so out of her teens, with long flaxen hair the color of a nicotine stain. As she bent over to unsnap the mayor's bra, Walter Peckman punched the stop button and the video recorder went fuzzy.

"Well, what do you think?" Peckman said, falling into his chair in a thick-bodied slump.

"Why me?" I asked.

"Why you? Because I can control you, Polo. And you're available. In fact, I made you available. You give me any shit and you'll be right back in the slammer."

"Five more months won't kill me."

Peckman nodded and slid forward in his seat. He was a big man, the kind that was probably a good athlete in school. But the muscles had long ago slid away to fat. He was in his late fifties and had the beef and bourbon complexion of a heavy drinker. The bald top of his head glistened under the strands of gray hair that were slicked across it. His eyes were a watery blue.

"Let's not bullshit each other, Polo. You want out. I don't care if you were in some white-collar, country club joint. You still want out. What the hell were you doing down there, anyway? You look like you just got back from a Hawaiian vacation."

"I'm the greenskeeper."

He arched an eyebrow? "Huh?"

"The greenskeeper. On the golf course."

Peckman drummed his fingers noiselessly on his desk. "Jesus. A man steals a quarter of a million dollars and they send him to jail and make a golf pro out of him."

"I didn't steal the money. I was just holding it as evidence."

"Yeah, yeah. The jury didn't buy that; don't try and sell it to me. You play ball with us on this and not only do you get out, but you can have these back."

He reached into a desk drawer, took out two plastic-coated cards, and flicked them toward me. I didn't have to look at them to know what they were. The yellow card was my private investigator's license. Now you've read books and seen movies where the poor private eye is in trouble with the cops and they threaten to have his license taken away and he gets all excited, right? Wrong. Let your fingers do a little walking though your local yellow pages under "Investigators" and out of the whole bunch you'll see that only about half of them list a license. The rest just rent an office, or work out of their basements, unlicensed. But the other card, the white one, the State of California license to carry a concealed pistol, revolver, or other weapon, that was something else. They are hard to get. Especially in this town. Especially if you've been convicted of a felony.

"You've got enough clout to get these back? No questions asked?"

Peckman gave me a smile no thicker than a razor blade. "Son, I've got more clout than you could ever use. You help us with this and your worries are over."

He was probably right. Peckman was sort of a junior kingmaker in California politics. Former state senator, former congressman, former chairman of the State Democratic Party. He had helped a lot of people get into, and kept a lot of people out of, public office—and had made an excellent living at it. It was no secret that he was grooming Barbara Martin for bigger and better things.

Peckman stood and walked over to a well-stocked bar. "Whiskey okay for you?"

"Fine." I glanced around. It was a nice room. The kind they don't build anymore: high ceiling, old burnished oak paneling, old comfortable padded-leather chairs, a thick green rug that Peckman must have brought in himself—it looked too new and too expensive for the city to have provided out of the recent so-called austerity budgets. The walls were cluttered with photographs of Peckman standing next to, or shaking hands with, politicians and celebrities. Peckman's official title was assistant to the mayor, but he was more than that, and generally considered the second most powerful man in city government; and as such I guess he rated a plush office right next to his boss.

He poured two hefty measures into old-fashioned glasses, no ice, no water, and handed me one.

"In an hour or so I'm supposed to be getting a phone call, Polo. I'll be told where to make a delivery. A delivery of thirty thousand dollars in cash."

"For the videotapes?"

"Yeah, for the tapes and some pictures. You're going to be the bagman."

"It's not enough."

Peckman scratched his jaw thoughtfully. "Yeah, I don't think so either. I think it's kind of a feeling-out deal. That's why I want you to deliver the money. Then I want you to find out who made the tape." He pulled an envelope from his suit jacket and dropped it into my lap. "And these pictures. Find out who took them and just what the hell they want."

I thumbed through the photographs. They were standard 35mm prints. There were an even dozen of them, all of Barbara Martin in various stages of undress with the same two youngsters who were in the videotape.

4

I took a tentative sip of the whiskey. It had been a long time between drinks, and straight shots before eleven in the morning had never been my thing anyway. "When were the pictures taken?"

"Four days ago."

"Where?"

"The mayor has a little place up in the wine country. St. Helena. Goes up there for the weekend every once in a while to get away from everything."

"It looks like something followed her up there this time." I studied the pictures. Mayor Barbara Martin was an attractive woman in her early forties. She was photographed in several different lingerie costumes that all looked like they'd been ordered out of a Frederick's of Hollywood catalog. The prints were all clear, well lighted, some taken in the bedroom, others in what looked like a living room, and three in a kitchen.

"These were all taken at the St. Helena place?" I said.

"Yep."

I took another pull at the whiskey. I knew that as mayor, Martin had access to a police bodyguard around the clock. "Where were the cops?"

"You've been out of circulation too long, Polo. The mayor and the police department are feuding. She refused to grant them a raise and fired what they considered to be a good chief and we thought was a rummy. Caused a lot of hard feelings. For all I know, they were the ones that set this up."

He read the look of disbelief on my face.

"Don't think it couldn't happen." He reached into a

walnut humidor, selected a cigar, then made a ceremony of clipping the cigar's end with a desktop cutter in the style of a guillotine. "Not too long ago an ex-cop, a supervisor, shot and killed the then mayor of San Francisco in the very next room. Then he calmly walked down the hallway and executed a fellow supervisor. So don't tell me that cops couldn't be involved in this."

The Dan White shootings of Mayor George Moscone and Supervisor Harvey Milk were still an open wound in the City. After the jurors' decision to slap White's hand, there had been a riot that threatened to burn down City Hall itself. Emotions ran high in the police department, spurred on by a few die-hard, gung-ho types who actually thought White was justified in what he did. It wasn't the main reason I'd left the department, but it was a contributing factor. There was a change you could almost feel, a loss of confidence, respect, pride. The White verdict, following the ill-fated police strike, seemed to gut the department. I used to love going to work, working overtime, sometimes with pay, sometimes to just finish the job. It was a game, the good guys against the bad guys. But the job changed. What the hell, the world changed. Still, I couldn't see any cop getting involved in something like this just because Martin knocked down a raise and fired a chief.

I picked up the pictures again. "She doesn't seem to be complaining very much. How did they get to her?"

Peckman lit his cigar and waved the cloud of smoke away with backhanded paddle motions. "You tell me. She left her office on Friday afternoon and drove straight up to St. Helena. She was meeting someone, but she won't tell me who—though I've got a pretty good idea who it was." He drained his glass and walked over to refill it. "Hell, she's human and her husband's been dead for over two years now. Anyway, she got there, and whoever she was expecting called and said he couldn't make it. She decided to stay, read, relax, goof off. A van drives up, a young guy carrying flowers rings the bell. Same punk who's in the pictures. She thinks the flowers are from her friend who canceled out. She goes to get some money to give the kid a tip, and when she gets back, he's in the house, with two other guys and the young girl."

"She was all alone? No protection at all? Nobody was scheduled to stop by and check on her?"

Peckman shrugged his shoulders. "What the hell, she does it all the time. You've got to get out of the fishbowl once in a while or you'll go crazy. She had her dog, Wolfie, a little cockapoo, or something poo; he barked like hell until he saw the dog these assholes brought. A big Doberman. Wolfie took off like a scared rabbit. Hasn't been seen since. So they had the mayor. And no one expected to hear from her until Sunday."

"What did they use on her?"

"I don't really know. They kept making her smoke cigarettes. She says they had a real strong pungent smell. Really stunk, not just grass. They held her nose, clamped down on her jaw to keep the smoke in. After a while she says she felt just like a zombie. Did anything they asked her to, just didn't feel like fighting back."

"It sounds like Angel-Mary. Marijuana laced with angel dust. That's dangerous stuff. Didn't you do a blood test? Urinalysis?"

"No, I told you, we didn't want any contact with the cops, crime lab, nobody. She saw her family doctor, but didn't tell him what actually happened, just that she wasn't feeling well. No other contacts. You're solo on this Polo."

"So all you know is that they want thirty thousand dollars. For openers."

"Yeah, for openers. Somebody called me yesterday morning. Told me to have the money ready today, by eleven." He flicked ash on the carpet and scattered it with a deft sideways movement of his shoe. "That's why I got you sprung from good old Lompoc Federal Prison. You were a pretty bright young guy until you got all screwed up with Uncle Sam. I want you to handle this. Find these bastards and get rid of them."

Peckman's face was getting redder and redder as he spoke. All of a sudden, my nice quiet bunk at Lompoc was looking good to me. "Get rid of them? I'm not Dirty Harry or some underground hit man."

Peckman made a movement with his chin and a clicking noise of the sort that encourages horses. "I'm not stupid, Polo. I just want you to take care of it. Barbara can't have this hanging over her head for the rest of her life. For all I know, these jerks will bleed us dry and then sell the stuff to *Penthouse* or *Hustler* or some other jerk-off outfit. We'll pay, but I want guarantees. You dig around, use your connections. Maybe they're freelance, maybe they're Mafia. Find out. You know some of those people."

"Some of those people? You mean my uncle? He's a

8

small-time bookie. What the hell would he know about any of this?"

"Dig around, that's all I'm asking." He frowned, hesitated, and for a moment seemed to be searching for words. "Barbara's a lady. A real class lady. She's already had some hard knocks in life. She doesn't deserve this."

Peckman got the call a little after eleven. I listened in on an extension phone. The voice was male, soft, and had a steely insistence.

The instructions were simple enough. Go to the Montgomery Street lobby of the Bank of America Building, near the cigar stand, and wait by the telephone booths.

I had to admit the idea wasn't too bad. No dark, lonely meeting places in back alleys. No dropping the money off in a garbage can at some secluded beach. What I liked most about it was that there didn't seem to appear to be much of a chance for bodily injury. My body.

The rose-granite-skinned Bank of America Building is the tallest structure in the City's rapidly changing skyline. Peckman had entrusted me with a black overnight bag stuffed with fifty- and hundred-dollar bills. He said the amount was thirty thousand dollars; I hadn't bothered to count it. There is a group of six open pay telephones directly across from the magazine stand. The phones are of a nice modern design that blends in well with the rest of the building but doesn't permit much privacy. One of the phones had an official-looking OUT OF ORDER sign hanging from the receiver. I positioned myself in front of it and picked it up on the first ring.

9

"You're prompt. Good. Now you are being watched, so follow my instructions precisely. No funny stuff. Don't try taping this conversation. Hang up and go to the elevators. Take the first one available and push the buttons for each floor. Do this for each elevator you use and go all the way to the top. At one of the stops you'll see a small rubber mat in front of the elevator door. When you see it, put the money alongside the mat and continue up to the top floor. If you try to call anyone, or stop to talk to anyone on the way to the elevator, or if you don't continue all the way up, I'll distribute the pictures all over the fucking state. That's a promise. Now get going."

He hung up before I could even say good-bye.

I rode the escalator up to the main floor, where the elevators are located. The building has four separate banks of elevators, each with eight individual elevators, four to each side. The first group travels from the first to the fifteenth floor. The next group handles passengers who want to get off between sixteen and twenty-six, the third from twenty-seven to thirty-nine, and the final bank goes from the fortieth to the final stop, floor fifty-two.

I dutifully stepped into the first available box and began pushing every button from two to fifteen. There were eight or nine people in the elevator with me. They gave me some strange looks, but nobody said anything.

I got off at fifteen. No sign of a mat yet, so I walked around the corridor to the elevators for the next series of stops. I lucked out here. Only two passengers. I again pushed all the buttons. One of the passengers, a middle-aged woman carrying a McDonald's lunch bag, tapped me on the shoulder.

"What the hell are you doing?" she asked angrily.

"Sorry, ma'am. State elevator inspector. Just checking the cable stress at stop area." I had no idea what any of that meant, but it sounded reasonable and made me feel slightly less foolish. Still no mats.

The elevator I picked up on the twenty-seventh floor was jammed and half the floor buttons were already pushed. I pushed the rest and gave the state inspector spiel again. Somebody standing in back shouted out a loud "Bullshit." I had to agree with him.

People were getting on and off at the next stops, and I had to struggle to stay up front where I could see the doors open. When they opened on the thirty-fourth floor, it was there. A small red rubber mat, the kind you put on the floorboard of the family sedan. I leaned out and placed the money bag alongside the mat. There was no one in the area, but I could see a red mat in front of each of the other seven elevator doors.

By now I'd had enough of the every-floor business, so I took the next ride all the way to the top, which happens to be the very exclusive, very expensive, members-only Bankers' Luncheon Club. After five o'clock it miraculously turns into the nonprivate, nonexclusive, but very expensive Carnelian Room.

I went straight to the bar and confidently ordered a bourbon and water. "I'm Mr. Ford's guest," I said to the bartender, figuring there had to be at least one banker named Ford in the business. Apparently there was. I got the drink.

2

Peckman's limousine was purring at the curb at the corner of Pine and Montgomery streets. His driver took me back to City Hall. Peckman was waiting nervously in his office. I told him how the money drop had gone.

"He didn't say anything about when he'd contact me again?"

"Not a word."

"How about you sticking around for a bit, Polo? Just in case he calls."

Lunch consisted of a saran-wrapped, tasteless ham and cheese sandwich and a Coke. Even prison cuisine was better than that.

I killed time by running the videotape. Peckman would come in and out of his office every now and then, always making sure he locked the door when I was there by myself. Like the still pictures, the tape was professionally done. Clear graphics, no shadows, no shaky camera angles. Mayor Martin was the featured player, but I was more interested in her companions. The boy had a sullen, arrogant manner about him. More importantly he had some nice tattoos: one on his forearm of a snake crawling up toward his bicep; the other on his chest, a flower, maybe a rose, it wasn't too clear. The snake looked like it was done by someone who knew what he was doing. The flower looked like an amateur job, like the kind that's done in prison with a heated ballpoint pen.

The girl had a dazed, dreamy look in her eyes, sometimes staring straight at the camera as if she was trying to make love to it.

Most of the activity took place on a brass-framed, king-sized bed.

On one of Peckman's visits he handed me an envelope.

"This is Barbara's statement."

"Good. I'd like to keep a couple of the still pictures."

"No way, Polo. No pictures leave this office!"

I took two of the pictures over to his desk and fidgeted one of them around in one of those hole punchers, the kind that put two holes in a piece of paper so you can place them neatly onto fasteners and file them away. I centered the mayor's face and punched it out. I handed the finished product to Peckman, then did the same thing to the next picture.

"There's no way anyone could recognize the mayor now. I'll need the pictures of the two kids. And the key to her place in St. Helena."

Peckman scrutinized the pictures closely, grunted his approval, and handed them back to me.

"Why do you want the keys?"

"The scene of the crime. Has anyone been there since the incident?"

"Just me. The bastards cleaned up after themselves pretty good. Clean as a whistle. I could even smell the ammonia they used."

"I'd still like to check it out. They could have bugged the place. Maybe that's how they knew she was there and that her boyfriend canceled his date."

"Okay," he agreed. "I'll get you a key. Where will you be staying?"

"My place, 742 Green."

Peckman scribbled the address down on a notepad. "What's your phone number?"

"I've been Uncle Sam's guest for the past seven months, remember? I'll call the phone company, but, knowing them, it'll take a couple of days to get the phone hooked up."

"I'll handle that. We've got to communicate. I want you checking in every few hours. No telling when these assholes will call again."

The next time Peckman left the room, I opened the bottom of the hole puncher and fished out the two circles showing Barbara Martin's head from the little bits of white and yellow paper and put them in my wallet. I also helped myself to one of Peckman's cigars, and when I saw the band said MONTE CRUZ HABANA, I grabbed six of them and stuffed them in my coat pocket. Once a thief, always a thief, they say.

Martin's statement was neatly typed out on heavy bond paper. Her description of the two kids in the pictures was limited, but she described the other two men as follows:

> #1—White, tall, over six feet. Bald, except for a bit of hair around the ears. (Shaves head?) Late thirties. Large droopy mustache, very black, like his eyebrows. (Dyes it?) Heavily muscled. (Weight lifter?) Suntanned. Strong, authoritative voice. Definitely in charge. (I think the others were afraid of him).
> #2—Oriental. Most probably Filipino. Early thirties. Tall (almost same height as #1). Thin. Longish dark hair. Pockmarked face, especially the nose. Cameraman.

She also listed the dog. She heard the big guy call him "Satan" once. She didn't hear any other names. The van was beige, old-looking. The flowers were a dozen roses.

The one thing she didn't mention was the name of the person she was supposed to meet for the weekend. Apparently that was going to be off limits to me.

When five o'clock rolled around and we hadn't heard anything from the blackmailers, I told Peckman we should call it a day. I also told him I'd need a little seed money to get my investigation going.

"How much?"

"A couple of thousand should do it?"

"A couple of thousand? That much?"

"You just handed over thirty thousand to a complete stranger. What's a couple more going to hurt. I'm going to have to spend money to get results. Of course, it'd be a lot cheaper to use the cops."

He reluctantly agreed, left the room again, and came back with the cash. This time I did count it. We parted with a handshake, and I made my way down the marble steps, through the magnificent City Hall rotunda, and out onto Polk Street. The afternoon wind had kicked up and the cool gray fog was rolling in. It was a welcome sight. A squadron of pigeons came out of the clouds and settled down in Civic Center Plaza. Even the pigeons looked good to me as they cockily strutted between the well-dressed attorneys and the heavily bundled street people who turned the Plaza into a campground every night. Some of those same pigeons would wind up over an open fire tonight, or in a pan over a single hot plate in some poor soul's one-room apartment. The turkey of the poor. Survival until the next Social Security check came in.

I was on my own now. No chauffeured limousine. Aside from the big hotels, City Hall is one of the few places in town where you can usually find a taxi.

I gave the driver my address and forgave his snarly "yeah, yeah" and sat back in the cracked vinyl seat and enjoyed the view. Cabbies are always hoping to pick up a fare to the airport, a good twenty-five-dollar trip. Anywhere else they treat like a waste of their time.

My flat on Green Street was my ace in the hole. In the prime of North Beach, two full six-room units, the upper, mine, even had a view of the bay, (if you stood on a stepladder or went up to the roof). I'd inherited the place from my parents, and it was the one asset my ex-wife and the government hadn't yet pried away. The lower unit was rented to an eighty-seven-year-old woman who showed every indication of outliving me. Mrs. Damonte had lived there since my father bought it. Realtors told me that I could easily rent the lower unit for twelve hundred to fourteen hundred dollars a month. She paid three hundred, which barely covered the taxes, but I wasn't about to try and budge her.

I could see her peeking out through lace curtains as I paid off the cabbie. She opened her chained door a crack as I walked past and asked in Italian if I was back for good.

I told her I hoped so and that it was good to see her, answering back in Italian, surprised that the language came back so easily.

Mrs. Damonte nodded her head a half inch. For her that was quite a greeting.

I let myself into my flat and began opening windows to let in some fresh air. The plants looked well watered, everything neat and clean, well dusted. Good old Mrs. Damonte again. I opened the refrigerator, empty except for a jar of olives and ice. Can you tell me how in the hell running one refrigerator and a light in the hall can run up an electric bill of thirty-two dollars a month? I always looked forward to mail in prison. Even the bills. But thirty-two smackers for an icebox and one light? Was Mrs. D. throwing parties up here? Sneaking up to watch the TV? I built myself a martini, took a pleasurable sip, then reminded myself to go slow. There are a lot of things you miss while you're in prison. The obvious, of course—sex and just plain freedom. But it's the little things that get to you. One was a long bath and shower. I took care of that first, then put a vintage Sinatra record on the phonograph and dressed leisurely in tan slacks, tan turtleneck sweater,

17

and a brown and tan check sport coat. No more gray for a while. I finished the last ice-melted drops of the martini and headed out for some nightlife.

One of the great things about living in North Beach is that you don't have to travel very far to find some excellent restaurants. I walked two blocks to La Felce and ordered pasta-pesto and veal saltimbocca, washing it down with a nice Valpolicella. Remember what I said about missing the little things in prison? Well, with me it was garlic. When you're a Sicilian and your mother raises you on the stuff all your life, you go a day or two without it and you get withdrawals. My mom thought that garlic was the universal antidote. She put it in everything but the coffee. Got a cold? Rub raw garlic on your chest. Flu? Eat raw garlic. High blood pressure? More garlic. I often wondered what would happen if Pop told her he had hemorrhoids.

While I ate, I went through Barbara Martin's statement again. Two men, one boy, one girl, and a dog. Which would be the easiest to find? The big guy certainly seemed to be the leader, but there really wasn't much information on him. The Oriental with the pockmarked face was a possibility. A cameraman and, judging from the quality of the video and the stills, probably a professional. The two kids in the pictures seemed the best bet for now, though average-looking kids into drugs and willing to do a porno with willing or unwilling partners were about as scarce as 49er fans at Candlestick Park.

When I'd used the last scrap of sourdough French bread to lap up the last drop of veal sauce, my plate looked as though a dog had licked it clean. I waddled out of the restaurant feeling better, and several pounds heavier, than I had in seven months.

I stopped at The Café on Columbus Avenue. It had no other name, just The Café, a small bar with a glistening chrome espresso maker and a few bottles of wine and imported beer visible behind an old varnished wooden bar.

I settled onto one of the barstools and spoke to the man behind the counter. "Pee Wee in?"

He was a big hulking guy in his fifties with a mop of curly gray hair, a flattened nose, and hard black eyes. His white shirt sleeves were rolled up, revealing thick, hairy wrists.

"Non comprendo," he said.

I answered back in Italian and asked if he would kindly inform Signor Polo that his nephew wished to see him.

He studied me briefly, then nodded and walked from behind the plank to an unmarked door at the rear of the room.

There were several card tables in the main section of The Café. One was occupied by three elderly gentlemen, all neatly dressed in pressed work pants, Pendleton shirts, and leather boots. It seemed to be the semiofficial uniform of all the retired Pisans in the neighborhood. I could remember my father wearing the same outfit on weekends.

They apparently figured that if the bartender hadn't bounced me out I was okay, because the card game started up again.

The bartender came back, placed a glass of red wine in front of me, and said, *"Un momentino."*

I sipped the wine and studied the posters that covered The Café's walls. They were all of boxers in various fight poses, advertising bouts of long forgotten warriors, their gloved fists protecting their faces, which were scowling out at their foes. One of the fighters looked like the bartender would have about thirty years ago.

"Hey, Nicky, how are you, boy?"

My uncle patted me on the back. He looked the same as when I had last seen him, which must have been three years ago. He was about my height, just a shade over six feet. He'd gotten the name Pee Wee because his brother, my father, was six feet three. He was immaculately dressed as usual, a light pearl gray suit, white shirt, solid black tie. His hair was as dark as his polished loafers, and I wondered if both were the result of frequent touchups.

He was a handsome man, the face unlined for his age, which had to be close to sixty. "Your brother never worked a day in his life," my mom would always say, and Pop would answer back, "Don't you think running away from the cops is hard work?"

"Good to see you, Nicky," he said, straddling the stool next to mine.

"Good to see you, uncle. You look well."

He laughed. "And you too, considering your recent address. You got out a little early, no?"

"A little. But I have to earn it."

"Ah, a deal was made, eh?" His gray eyes iced over. "Something to do with me?"

20

"No. Not at all. I came because I could use a little advice."

He spread out his hands. "What are uncles for?"

"I was let out of prison to help someone. Someone important. There were pictures taken. Compromising pictures. Professional-looking pictures."

"And your important person, he somehow thinks what? That organized crime is involved and that I would have knowledge of it?"

"That was mentioned. I explained that it was not possible. Still, I thought you might have heard of something. The cameraman was an Oriental."

"An Oriental?" He laughed loud enough for the men at the table to stop their card game momentarily. "Tell your important friend to check with the Chinese Mafia, or the Japanese Mafia, or the Filipino Mafia, or the Vietnamese Mafia. I tell you *Niccolò*, anytime a couple of punks get together on a street corner nowadays, they start a gang—the Blacks, the Latins, there is no organization, just a few punks, but they see the movies, the television, they want to be *capo de capos*, like it is in New York or Chicago." He shook his head sadly. "I tell you it is getting hard for a respectable man to make an honest living in this town anymore."

"How is business?"

He shrugged his elegant shoulders. "*Mezzo e mezzo*. This is important to you?"

"Very."

"Then I will ask around."

"There was another man involved. White, big,

21

maybe a weight lifter, bald head, mustache, in his thirties. He has a dog. A Doberman named Satan."

"Satan, eh? It sounds like the right name. Call me in a couple of days."

I stopped at a drugstore and bought a roll of Clorets and a Binaca spray to help camouflage the smell of the garlic, then pointed my feet in the direction of Union Street and Perry's, probably still the number-one drinking establishment dedicated to the fact that all men and all women are not created equal and sometimes the nonequals like to get together and interchange parts for a short time. I mean I wasn't lying when I said that I missed garlic, but the ninety-nine percent of the time garlic wasn't on my mind, women were.

I elbowed my way through a mass of herringbone jackets, stepped on numerous penny loafers, and finally found a spot at the bar next to an attractive lady with long dark silky hair that swished around her shoulders when she turned to talk to the girl on the next stool. I edged closer, tipping her arm slightly and spilling part of her drink on the bar. I apologized profusely and offered to buy her a fresh drink. Thus started the ritual ceremony of courtship in the "City That Knows How." She admired my tan, which I told her came from a two-week vacation in Hawaii. I admired her dress, which she said was new, "first time out of the closet," which was the opening she used to ask me if I was bisexual. No. Into heavy drugs, "anything with needles?" No. And of course the dreaded herpes question. No again. We seemed both biologically and clinically matched, so the conversation over the next

22

couple of drinks returned to something approaching normalcy. I learned that her name was Nancy, that she was from Des Moines, had been in San Francisco for two years, loved it, except for the problem of finding straight, single, nondiseased men who were interested in more than just a one-night stand.

The bartender poured her last glass so full she had to bend over in order to sip without spilling the wine. While she was bobbing in Chablis, I got the bartender to call for a cab, and within a half an hour we were at her apartment, a two-room affair decorated with throw rugs and Clint Eastwood posters.

The sex was cold, impersonal, mechanical, and absolutely wonderful. The second time was better, and by the time the morning alarm went off and we once again started groping at each other, Nancy was beginning to get the idea she'd found a sexual superman. Absence does make more than the heart grow fonder, friend.

She made coffee and eyed me anxiously as she showered and dressed for work, probably afraid that I would decide to camp there for the day and when she got home all her Clint Eastwood posters would be gone. I dressed quickly and we exchanged phone numbers, promising each other that we'd try and get together in the next few days, neither of us believing that the other was serious. I was. Nancy was bright, attractive, and had a perverse sense of humor. She was almost perfect, her main drawback being that she worked for a law firm and was going to law school three nights a week. You know the old gag? How can you tell when your lawyer is lying to you? When his lips move. Well, I'd seen too many lips move in my time, the last pair costing me seven months in the Crossbar Hotel.

Nancy had a friend picking her up for work, so I lit one of Peckman's Havana cigars and started marching back to my flat. I already mentioned the problems with cabs in the City. The buses are even worse. They run in packs, like wolves. You wait forty minutes for one, then all of a sudden they start pulling in bumper to bumper. Once you're onboard, if you don't have the exact change, the driver will kick you off. Even if you get by him, you have to risk mingling with the rest of the passengers. Your best bet is to find someone who looks like Charles Bronson and stay close. Walking and the cable cars are really the only two ways to go, because if you drive your own car, you'll soon find out that there is never a place to park. Unless of course you happen to be driving a police car, something I planned to take care of as soon as possible.

I stopped at Danilo's bakery and picked up several pastries smothered with almonds and custard, bought the morning paper, and got home a few minutes after nine. There was an envelope pinned to my front door with a message scrawled across it: "Your phone works. Use it!" Inside the envelope was a key and a map to Martin's place in St. Helena along with an explanation of how to turn off her burglar alarm.

Peckman was right. The phone did work. The man had clout with a capital C. Getting me sprung wasn't much of a deal, but to get the phone company off their poles that quick was really something.

I called Peckman. He was in his usual good mood.

"Where the fuck have you been?"

"Working. Any word from the bad guys?"

"Nothing. I want to hear from you every few hours, Polo. With results."

There was a click and the buzz of a disconnected line. No good-byes. Just like in the movies.

I started a pot of coffee and combed through the car rental ads in the phone book, made four calls before I found what I was looking for, then called for a taxi.

The cab driver surprised me. I only had to wait twenty minutes for him and the guy was cheerful. Our first stop was Weeks Cameras on Market Street. I explained what I needed and was told that because they would first have to make negatives from the prints, then crop them, it would take a full week to get the work done. The time kept dwindling down about a day for each ten-dollar bill I laid on the counter top. When we reached eighty bucks, it was agreed that I could have the prints by five that evening.

The cabbie swung down Sixth Street, onto the freeway, and headed south. No wonder he was smiling—we were going toward the airport.

The Acme car rental agency was the kind of operation that bought fleet cars from another agency after they had picked them up from Hertz. They had just what I was looking for, a three-year-old Ford Granada, beige, dented fenders, bent bumpers, and one cracked window. I paid off the cabbie, signed the rental forms, and drove to the Tanforan Shopping Center and purchased a red emergency light that plugged into the car's cigarette lighter, a CB radio microphone, and a three-foot radio whip antenna. I picked up a clipboard and some Scotch tape from a stationery store, and then it was back home for a few alterations on the Granada.

I taped the microphone cord under the dash, letting the mike sit on the front seat. The red light went next to it, along with the clipboard. Swapping the antennas was a bit more work than I thought it would be, but when I stood back and examined the car, it looked pretty good, though it was a shame that the rental agency had washed it. A few coats of grime, some cigarette butts on the floor, and a little dried vomit on the backseat and it would have been perfect, but you can't have everything.

I went inside, crawled under the kitchen sink, and, resisting the urge to say abracadabra or Ollie Ollie Oxen Free, worked the hinged panel that opened what I had always considered as a kid to be my father's secret hiding place. Pop was a brickmason, which was why the flat looked a little like Fort Apache. He was also a crackerjack carpenter, so he'd fixed up this little hideout to keep his valuables. His valuables in those days consisted of the good grappa he made in the cellar. Most bottles went quick, either by consumption or as gifts to friends. But he always stored a few back here behind the sink, along with his insurance papers, some of Mom's good jewelry, and gold coins. Being a curious and sneaky little brat, I'd found out about it and helped myself to a few slugs of the grappa now and then. Dad found out about it of course, leaking the word to Mom so that she could warn me and so that he wouldn't have to belt me. After that the jewelry and the gold coins stayed, but the grappa was moved to a locked closet in the basement.

I reached back behind the cabinets and pulled out a

26

large steel box. The box was covered with dust, which meant that this was one spot Mrs. Damonte hadn't discovered. I took my police inspector's badge, which I had thoughtfully forgot to turn in when I quit the department, and a small .25-caliber holstered Beretta automatic from the box. My mother's jewelry and Dad's gold coins were still there, carefully wrapped in heavy jeweler's cloth. There were three other guns in the box: the .357 Magnum Smith & Wesson I was issued when I joined the department and two strays that I had literally picked up along the way, a Colt .38 short-barreled revolver and an old Star automatic that had been made in Spain. I selected the Colt, then put a thousand dollars of the money that Peckman had given me, along with the two cut-out pictures of Barbara Martin's head, in the box and slid it back into its hiding place.

Carrying a gun is one highly overrated pleasure. Guns are heavy, clumsy, and messy. They're also dangerous. The Beretta had an ankle holster that slipped over the calf, and after an hour or so you kind of forgot about it. I strapped it on, got my coat, then brought the .38, along with a sharp-pointed knife, a wad of paper towels, and the Scotch tape, back out to the car. I carefully cut away the siding on the passenger side headrest, laying it open, then pulled out the stuffing. After covering the gun's barrel with a small strip of tape, I placed the .38 in the now hollow compartment. It took a few tries, but I finally got the right combination of stuffing and paper towels so that the headrest looked fairly normal. I resealed the headrest flap with the tape. It looked okay. You might notice it on a new car, but not on this baby.

Before becoming a guest of the federal government, I had an office on Market Street. All of my office furniture and files were now jammed into the flat's third bedroom. I dug around in one of the black metal filing cabinets and found the two items I wanted: a small bug detector called, of all things, the Hound Dog, and my handy-dandy fingerprint kit, a satchel-sized leather grip stuffed with dusting powders, glues, scissors, rulers, and magnifying glasses, none of which I'd ever used.

3

It was a fine, sunny day with just a few popcorn clouds drifting slowly across the sky. I sat back to enjoy the ride. Unfortunately, sitting back too far made a spring dig into my vertebrae. One thing the car did have was an AM/FM radio, so I zeroed in on KJAZ and listened to an old Miles Davis track as I crossed the Golden Gate Bridge. I followed Highway 101 through the emerald green hills of Marin, cut over through Sonoma, and then into the famed Napa Valley. The map Peckman had given me was simple enough to follow: through the old-fashioned Main Street of St. Helena, with its wonderful old three-ball streetlights, stately brick business district, and gingerbread Victorian houses, past the tunnel of elm trees leading to Christian Brothers Winery, then a left turn on Chardonnay Lane. The narrow two-lane blacktop wove around acres and acres of lush grapevines. The only sound was the zip of the tires on the road. I found a mailbox numbered 1927 and turned left onto a gravel path, the tiny stones pinging on the car's fenders. I'd gone a good half mile before I got a look at what Peckman had described as "a little place up in the wine country." The architecture was a blend of contemporary and California Spanish, with rough plaster walls and a curved red tile roof.

I coasted to a stop under a massive oak tree. Horseshoe-shaped stairs led to an impressive front entrance. Peckman's key slid easily into the lock. The burglar alarm was just inside the door, a simple electronic on-off switch. Simple, and useless if you're tricked into opening the door for the bad guys. The interior was all white walls, curved arches, and deep-mahogany plank floors. The furniture was modern: plastics, metal and glass. There was a green and white floral-patterned couch in the living room that I remembered from the photographs. The paintings on the walls all looked like original abstract oils in warm beiges, reds, and oranges. I pulled out the probe antenna on the Hound Dog and wandered around from room to room. Behind one door I found a full regulation-sized pool table, the brightly colored balls displayed on the green felt looking like a pop art poster.

The Hound Dog's meter stayed at a steady zero reading, no sign of any bugs. The kitchen was huge, with an aluminum, restaurant-capacity refrigerator and a double-oven, six-burner stove. The refrigerator would have been a perfect spot for fingerprints, so I gave it a dusting and peered through the magnifying glass just like I knew what I was doing. Nothing, not a spot. Peckman was right, you could smell the ammonia. I opened the fridge and found it stocked with a dozen different imported beers, a wide variety of California and French wines and champagnes, and some sausages and cheeses. I picked out a San Miguel dark and poured it into a nice tulip-shaped glass from one of the oak kitchen cabinets. All the glasses were crystal clear, not a sign of a print or even a dishwasher spot.

I found a closet holding a mop, a broom, and some cleaning materials, and rummaged around until I found an almost empty bottle of Windex and a can of all-purpose cleaner. I dusted them carefully for prints. No dice.

There was a scratching sound from the back of the house. I froze, dropped to one knee, grabbed the Beretta, and then made my way cautiously to a Dutch-windowed door in the rear of the kitchen. The window looked out to a vast open grass area, the grass long, uncut, and showing numerous brown spots. I opened the door and found the culprit, a tiny ball of fur shaking in excitement. Martin's dog.

"Hey, fella, come here." The dog backed away, growling lightly. He looked like he'd been in a fight with a mouse and came out the loser. I tried to remember his name. What the hell was it? Wolf? Wolfie. That was it. I called him by his name, and he inched closer, finally surrendering with a sigh as I scratched him behind his ears. I picked him up, holding him as far away as I could. Little Wolfie couldn't weigh more than a couple of pounds, but he smelled like he'd been mating with skunks.

"Come on, Wolfie, let's eat." There was some dog food in one of the cabinets. Wolfie went through a whole can without stopping. I settled for some cheese and crackers and the beer. When he was through eating, I dumped him in the kitchen sink, gave him a quick bath, and wrapped him in a couple of dish towels. Polo's good deed for the day. Now back to work, or whatever the hell it was I thought I was doing.

A lazy, curving stairway serpentined upstairs. I poked the Hound Dog into each room, checking each telephone along the way, and ended up in the master bedroom. It looked exactly as it had in the pictures, only much neater. The pale ivory carpet was plush from a recent vacuuming. The furniture was all white with gold trim, the walls lavender. The king-size bed was covered in a heavy silk quilt, and the brass headboard was of a modern-Oriental design with crisscrossed square tubing. I dusted the brass thoroughly, remembering seeing several hands and feet tangled up between the openings. Again, nothing. Nothing but the lingering smell of ammonia.

Little Wolfie trailed alongside me everywhere I went. He wasn't about to get kicked out of his own house twice. I had one more hope of picking up a print. After the party they had gone to a lot of trouble to clean up. Who did the work? Being chauvinistic, no-good assholes, they probably had the girl do it, right? The head bad guy, Baldy, he might supervise, but would he get his hands dirty? The other guy, Pockmarks, he was probably busy with his cameras and video machines. The boy, he looked like he was hired for one thing only, the length of his genitalia. That left the girl. The master bathroom was exactly like the rest of the house—big, expensive, and slightly overdone: gray tile, a sunken tub, a rounded glass stall shower, double basin, the plumbing fixtures all gold and shaped like little dolphins. I went to my last hope, lifted the cover, and dusted. Bingo! Three

32

prints right under the lid. Who ever would have thought that a toilet seat could look that lovely. I didn't trust my expertise in lifting the prints with tape. The seat was fastened with two loose plastic bolts, so I simply unscrewed them and took off the whole seat, then went back to the bed, borrowed one of the pillow slips, and gently slipped in my prize.

I checked the bedroom telephone, one of those plastic and curly brass jobs, for bugs, then called Peckman. He answered on the second ring.

"I've got some good news, unless you took a leak in the master bathroom when you were up here."

Peckman's voice dripped icicles. "I could use some good news. Barbara's got a new batch of pictures. And a demand. Give up the Senate race."

"Give up the Senate race? That was it? No more money?"

"That was enough. Now what did you find?"

I told him about the prints. "I'll have them checked out." He started to protest. "Don't worry, nothing official. How was this demand sent?"

"In the mail. Plain envelope. Postmarked in the City, sent to her home address."

"I'd like to see everything—the pictures, the letter, the envelope."

"It'll have to wait. I'm leaving for Sacramento right now. I won't be back until tomorrow at the earliest. I've got a hunch who's behind this now. Dirty bastards, I never thought they'd stoop to anything like this."

"Then I want to see you as soon as you get back. I

want—" Wolfie laid his head on my shoe. "Oh, another thing, I've got the mayor's dog. Where shall I take it?"

"Wolfie?" Peckman chuckled. "The little fart showed up, huh? Great watchdog. Drop him off at Barbara's place." He gave me the address. "And Polo, just drop the dog off, don't bother the lady."

4

So Wolfie ended up in an empty cardboard box and slept all the way back to San Francisco. The mayor's house in Seacliff made her country place look like poverty row. Three stories of stained-glass windows, old bricks, old wood, and old money. I carried Wolfie over grass so tightly cut it looked like Astroturf. In San Francisco, where most single-family dwellings got by with a twenty-five-foot frontage, this place looked like a Texas ranch. The front door was opened by a very proper-looking gentleman in a very proper-looking dark suit. He was in his fifties. Picture David Niven with no mustache and twenty pounds on him. He accepted Wolfie's box gingerly, thanked me in a clipped British accent, and invited me in.

I cooled my heels for a couple of minutes under a shower of crystal hanging from a priceless antique chandelier suspended from a high, frescoed ceiling.

The butler came back and gestured to me with one finger, and I followed him, my heels clicking on the travertine marble floor. He opened the door to an enormous room with ancient heavy wooden furniture standing in museum arrangements around the walls, under paintings picturing horses and men in red coats chasing off after foxes. A glorious Kerman carpet covered most of the buffed parquet floor.

Barbara Martin was bent over in front of a massive open fireplace. She stood, turned, and greeted me. Wolfie was stuck safely under one arm.

"Thank you, Mr. Polo. Thank you so much for bringing Wolfie home to me."

She was taller than I thought, with an erect carriage. Her cheeks were flushed. They were the high cheekbones of a fashion model, cheekbones that would carry her well through life's changing cycles. She wore a stylish beige dress and pearls. She was a classically beautiful woman, and it was hard to equate her with the caricature on the videotape.

"My pleasure," I said. "He looks happy to be home."

Wolfie squirmed a bit, and she put him down and he ran over to me. I bent down and scratched him behind his ears.

"Walter told me that you were . . . being very helpful, Mr. Polo."

From the fireplace came a series of cracks, a bright moment of flame, and the smell of sap as the log caught fire.

She picked up a glass filled with ice and a clear liquid from a coffee table, then pointed to a drink tray. "Why don't you help yourself to a drink."

The liquor was in tall crystal decanters with little silver tags hanging from chains identifying the Scotch, bourbon, gin, and vodka. The vodka looked pretty low in comparison to the others. I picked up a glass and scooped some ice from a silver bucket. The ice was pretty well melted and looked like it had been there awhile. I poured some Scotch into the glass and raised it to her in a wordless toast.

She slumped into an overstuffed couch like a runner whose legs had given out and took a sip of her drink. I sat at the far end of the couch. We were quiet for a long, uncomfortable minute, then I stupidly said, "That's a beautiful place you have in St. Helena." It was one of those times when you want to snatch the words back as you're saying them, but it was too late.

Her face clouded over and she crossed her arms, hugging herself in a protective, virginal gesture.

I dove back into my drink, trying to think of something a little more delicate to add to the conversation.

Her voice was barely audible when she swiveled to face me. Her eyes were a deep, faraway blue. "I hope . . . I hope you can help me, Mr. Polo. I'd like . . . I'd like all of them punished." She was slurring her words now. "Every last one punished, do you understand?"

"I'll do my best, Mrs. Martin."

She giggled, a strange, high-pitched giggle. "Under the circumstances, I think you can call me Barbara."

She turned those eyes on me again. The blue reminded me of the color of a very inviting pool on a hot day. You could dive into those eyes and never want to come up again.

37

I finished my drink, gave Wolfie a final pat, and exited as gracefully as I could.

From the sublime to the ridiculous. I left the rarefied atmosphere of Seacliff, drove down California Street, right on Gough past the controversial architecture of St. Mary's Cathedral, briefly onto the freeway, off on Seventh Street, and parked in a red zone on Harriet, next to the Hall of Justice. My rental special mixed in perfectly with a half dozen or so illegally parked unmarked police cars.

Now if you've never been to San Francisco and you're planning to come and see the sights, one of the sights you definitely want to cross off your list, unless you're forced to go there because you've been beaten, robbed, mugged, raped, or arrested for soliciting, is the Hall of Justice; a mammoth concrete-block building resembling a child's Tinkertoy nightmare. A dingy gray, streaked with brownish rivulets where the rust from window frames has washed down the walls, it covers a full city block in the South of Market area, an area which, blessedly, usually escapes the eyes of weary tourists.

As bad as it is outside, the inside is worse, because that's where the weirdos are. The first floor is taken up by the Traffic Bureau, Southern Station, and a few court rooms. The second and third floors are jammed with more courtrooms, the Probation Department, and the district attorney's office. The detective bureaus are on the fourth and fifth floors, the jail on the sixth. The elevators that feed the entire complex are centrally located, so some poor guy that just got robbed and beaten last night is likely to ride up to court in the elevator with the very

38

same gentleman, or more likely gentle*men*, out on bail, who massaged his scalp with a crowbar.

The Crime Lab is on the third floor, right across from the Sexual Assault Detail. If you're expecting a clean, well-lighted, antiseptic-smelling area with lots of scholarly-looking men in long white coats walking around smoking pipes, you came to the wrong place.

I found Harry Saito in his office, sitting behind a battered desk. The top, where it wasn't covered by Styrofoam coffee cups, manila folders, and evidence jars filled with foul-looking specimens, was tattooed with cigarette burns. Saito peered up at me and his eyes widened briefly. He was a small, spare man with skin the color of light tea. His shirt sagged to one side from the weight of a dozen varicolored pens and pencils packed in its pocket.

"I didn't hear anything about a jailbreak, Nick. How the hell did you get here?"

"Connections, Harry, connections. I need a favor."

"Shit, who don't? I'm busy. See me next week."

"Can't wait." I opened the pillowcase and carefully placed the toilet seat on top of the folders on his desk.

Saito leaned back in his seat and folded his arms across his chest. "You're a bad boy, Nick. No longer a cop. I can't do anything for you. What are you going to try and do? Bribe me?"

"Catch." I took one of Peckman's Havanas from my pocket and tossed it to Saito.

He caught it deftly, removed the plastic wrapper and studied it suspiciously, then let out a small sigh as he ran the cigar under his nose.

"Ah, Nick. I bribe easy. You could have got me for a Dutch Master. What do you need?"

"Under the front lid of the toilet seat are what look like three pretty good prints. I want you to run them, that's all."

"That's all? You got any more of these Cubans?"

I tossed him another cigar. "If the prints come out, run a make on the owner. The works. Criminal, motor vehicles, reports, everything. If this turns out to be anything, I'll get you a whole box of the damn cigars."

Saito rose to his full height, an inch or two over five feet, picked up the toilet seat, and shepherded me out of his office. "Come back in the morning. After ten. I'll have it by then."

I went back to the car and found the windshield blank. So far, the score was Polo 1, meter maids 0. I parked in front of a fire hydrant by Weeks Cameras, getting there just before they closed. They had done a good job. The close-ups of both the boy and the girl were as good as could be expected in five-by-seven blowups from a cropped negative. Now all I had to do was find them.

5

I started at the topless joints on Broadway, showing the pictures, giving a story about missing kids, parents just died, left a lot of money, that kind of thing. I must have interviewed thirty kids, all as young as the pair I was looking for, all better-looking. The response was always the same: "Who gives a shit?"

I worked my way down to the Tenderloin and hit the arcades, garishly lighted dumps advertising promises such as "Talk to a Naked Girl for a Dollar." The insides of these establishments were always darker than the outsides. There were racks of porno books catering to both gays and straights, everything from bondage to bestiality. Wonderful stuff. They should hold a contest: "Find one picture of a normally built man and woman doing it in the missionary position and win an all-expense-paid trip to the brothel of your choice."

You give your dollar bill to a surly-looking guy with his T-shirt rolled up to show his biceps and a snarl permanently stitched on his face. He hands you little brass tokens the size of a quarter, then you go into a room slightly larger than a phone booth. You shove your quarter in a slot, and then the lights go on behind a smudged window, a young lady comes out, sits on a plain old wooden chair. She's naked. Boy, what fun, huh? Most of them are under twenty, with pallid skin and pimples. The young lady says she'll talk to you about anything you want and that you can do anything you want on your side of the glass but they're not allowed to date the customers. But if you don't ask them for a date after the first few tokens, they figure you for a dud. A token lasts exactly a minute, so you have to talk pretty fast. I took my time, dropping lots of tokens and promising lots of money if they could help me locate the two poor babies in the pictures. All I got for my efforts was a dent in Peckman's expense money and a headache. After the first few interviews they all seemed to lump together: they all had a sameness to them, besides the blotchy skin, the vacant, muddy eyes, the needle marks on their arms and legs visible even through the dirty glass. It was the feeling of joylessness they gave off, even the ones that had a little spark and tried to hustle you for a few more tokens, or a date, or had tried to say they knew the people in the pictures but then broke down when you asked for specifics. They all had that tired, "what's the use" air about them.

It's a fact that in crashes involving airplanes, the pilot, be he commercial or private, will usually say, if he has a second or two before he rams into a mountain, an ocean, or good old Mother Earth, "Oh shit!" Famous last words. Why not? There's no time for an Act of Contrition or to be reborn, so "Oh shit" it is. These kids seemed to have a code phrase for everything: "Who gives a shit?" What a waste.

I finally had enough, picked up the evening *Examiner* and walked a few short blocks to Original Joe's, a good old San Francisco restaurant that somehow survives in the jungle of the Tenderloin, sat at the counter, and watched the cooks sweating over the open stoves as waiters called in their garbled orders. Two drinks, a half bottle of wine, veal sauté, and spaghetti pulled me out of my blues.

There was a light rain falling by the time I left the restaurant. The pimps sat huddled in their cars while the girls, boys, and boys dressed like girls tried to find an awning or a doorway that wasn't being used for any of a variety of purposes.

I decided to give the booth girls one more shot and hit the arcades on Turk Street, but an hour and thirty-five tokens later I gave up. The rain had quit, leaving the streets Vaseline shiny. I had left the Ford in front of another fire hydrant, and I smiled when I saw the clean windshield again. Then I heard the footsteps walking hurriedly, with a purpose. That sixth sense, or whatever it is, was telling me I was the purpose.

They were so close I didn't have time to bend down and reach for the Beretta. They were dressed similarly dark pants, dark leather jackets.

"Hey, buddy," the bigger of the two yelled. "How come you're looking for them people."

I recognized him as one of the token takers and went into my spiel about the parents dying and leaving some money, but I could tell they really weren't interested. They kept edging toward me, moving me away from the street and into a half-empty parking lot. The bigger one was doing all the talking. He was about my height, but thicker through the body. He had the eyes of a hunter—small, dark, and quick—and a nose that looked like it had taken a dive in a heavyweight fight. His partner was about the same age, mid-twenties, but shorter and thinner, with a complexion like gray stone.

"Here, take a look at these," I said, holding out the pictures, then I kicked the big one in the balls as hard as I could. He buckled over and I brought an elbow up in a short arc, catching him in the nose. I swiveled around, but not in time to avoid a glancing blow off the side of my skull. I struck out blindly, making contact, and saw the other one backing off a few steps, holding a pipe wrench above his shoulder. We circled each other warily.

"Drop that wrench, son, or I'm going to take it away from you and shove it up your ass."

He smiled back, showing huge teeth like a jack-o'-lantern. "When we get through with you, pretty boy, there'll be more than this pipe up your ass."

The big guy was struggling to his knees, blood streaming from his nose. I got behind him and aimed a kick to his kidneys as Lantern Teeth charged in once again. He was holding the wrench too high, and I had time to duck under his arm, bringing my left hand over the top of his forearm, then my right up to his elbow. There was a loud cracking sound as the arm broke. He dropped the wrench, then ran screaming out into the street, almost banging into a passing car. I kicked the wrench into the gutter and squatted down to the big one. He was moaning lowly.

"I think my nose is broke. Get me a doctor."

I grabbed his hair, a bad mistake, I found, as my hand slipped through pomade. I finally got a grip on his neck and pushed his face into the sidewalk. "Talk to me, friend, or when I get through with you, you won't have any nose at all."

"We were just askin' questions. We wasn't going to try anything."

I bounced his head on the cement. "Look, you were never pretty to begin with. One more time, or you're going to have a face like the Pillsbury Dough Boy. Who set you on me? Do you know the two people in the pictures?"

"Honest, honest, we were just trying to—"

I heard a police siren, not exactly an unusual sound for that time of the night in the Tenderloin district, but I didn't want to take the chance that they were coming my way. I got into the Granada and took off, driving a good six blocks before pulling to the curb. My hands were shaking. Two punks, sure. But two punks who could have easily dumped me and beaten me to a pulp. From now on, the Beretta was going to be in my pants pocket where I could get at it quicker. Were they just after a likely mark? Or had one of the girls recognized someone in the pictures and tipped them off? I started the car and headed toward home, gripping the wheel very hard. That way I couldn't tell if my hands were still shaking.

6

"Wooden matches," Harry Saito said. "Good wooden matches, that's what you should light Havanas with. Either that or a gold Dunhill, Nick."

"I take it you got the prints."

Saito beamed, his round face splitting into an almost obscene smile. "I sure did. And a rap sheet with a mug shot and a driver's license."

I gave him the last of Peckman's cigars. "This is on account. Let's see what you've got."

He stopped smiling as he dug through the enormous pile of folders on his desk, finally digging out the right one. Bingo. The same young Latin kid who'd been in the pictures with Barbara Martin was frowning at me from his mug shot. His name was Richard Moreno. His last arrest was for an assault at Taylor and O'Farrell, just a block or two from where the two punks hit me last night. I scanned his sheet, which showed several more arrests, but no convictions, for assault and pandering, all in the Los Angeles area. The computer printout from the Department of Motor Vehicles showed a local postal box for his address.

After leaving Saito's office I stopped at the Vice Squad and spotted the friendly face of Inspector Jack Ryan. Ryan was a tall, well-built guy with the map of Ireland on his face, except for a nose that was shaped like it should have been on the rider of a camel in the middle of the Sahara Desert. We swapped a few lies, then I dropped Moreno's mug shot and the five-by-seven glossy on his desk. "Ever run into this beauty?"

"Nah, not that I know of."

I showed him the picture of the girl. "He and this little lady have made a few pornos."

"She doesn't ring any bells either, Nick."

"Ever hear of a cameraman, Oriental guy with a heavily pockmarked face?"

"Hell, who ever sees the cameraman? We don't bother with this stuff anymore, unless there are young kids involved or someone is forced into it and makes a complaint."

I described the bald guy and his dog and got another negative from Ryan.

"What if I was interested in making, or investing in, a porno film, and I wanted to find some actors and a good cameraman. Who would I see?"

Ryan ran the index finger of his left hand along his nose. "I'd try Auntie Jill."

"Auntie Jill?"

He picked up a Rolodex from his desk and thumbed through the cards. "Auntie Jill used to be what they called a 'starlet' in Hollywood. The jobs started to get scarce, she tried to get into directing, got nowhere, so she made a few soft-porn films, then she started aging a wee bit and went into the production end. Here it is, Argonaut Productions. Jill Ashbury."

He pulled the card from the Rolodex and I copied down the information.

"She should open up to you. Use my name, she owes me a favor or two."

I thanked him and shook hands without asking just how he came into the favors.

The post office is funny. Tough to deal with. I had my police inspector's badge, but even if it was valid, I still would have a tough time getting any information out of them. J. Edgar Hoover reincarnated would have a tough time getting anything out of them. Like the phone company, they'd been burned too many times by the locals and the federalies. Mostly the federalies. Still, there's always a way.

The postal clerk at Rincon Annex, a short, round man with a sullen, pinched-in face and an "I've got twenty years in and ten more to go" civil-service slouch examined my subpoena with wary and bitter eyes.

"What do you want from me?" he asked.

I tapped the subpoena. "This is a civil case. *Doorknocker* v. *Universal Insurance*. Mr. Richard Moreno is a witness. We are subpoenaing him."

48

"So?"

"So the only address we have for him is postal box 9340 here at this branch. I want the address he put on his application when he got the box."

"So?"

I read the name off the tag on his dirty blue sweater. "So, Mr. Deamias, if you don't give it to me, then I'll just subpoena you, and you can explain to the judge why you wouldn't give it to me."

He grunted something unintelligible and slammed down the window. I spent the next ten minutes admiring the metal-grilled windows and wall murals. They just don't build post offices like they used to—solid walls, graceful arches, patriotic designs in the marble floors. Deamias finally came back, opening the window with a bang. He was smiling, so I knew I was in trouble.

"Here you are, sport. This is the only address we have for Mr. Moreno."

No wonder he was smiling. Moreno's address on the application form was for another postal box. In Cobb.

The map for northern California showed Cobb as a small dot situated, appropriately enough, on the top of Cobb Mountain; it was a good three-hour drive away. The interesting thing about it was that one of the ways to get there took you right through St. Helena.

The headline on the early edition of the *Examiner* stopped me in my tracks as I was leaving the post office: MAYOR QUITS SENATE RACE. There was a picture of Barbara Martin under the headline. She looked drawn and serious. The story said she had given the matter much

49

thought and figured she owed it to the people of the City and County of San Francisco to remain a full-time mayor. The reporter had hinted at possible health problems, which were vigorously denied by the mayor's assistant, Walter Peckman. It took several tries, but I finally got through to Peckman on the phone. He was obviously upset. We agreed to meet for a drink in two hours at Kimball's, a watering hole a couple of blocks away from City Hall.

That gave me plenty of time to look up good old Auntie Jill. The address Jack Ryan had given me for her turned out to be part of an old warehouse in the industrial center, right next to a firehouse. There wasn't a legal or illegal parking spot in sight. Some of the fire hydrants even had trucks double-parked in front of them. Where the hell are the cops when you need them.

I flashed my badge at a fireman leaning against the wall of the firehouse. He nodded and I pulled the Granada up onto the sidewalk. The cops and firemen in this town have a more or less "I'll help you when I can if you help me when you can" agreement. The strike a few years back had embittered the relationship, but since a good portion of the fire department was made up of ex-cops that had either gotten tired of police business or just got smart and switched jobs, the bond still held.

The fireman on watch was a big, fresh-faced, good-looking guy in his early thirties.

"I'll leave the keys in the car in case you have to move it," I told him.

"No problem. You going next door?"

"Right."

"They're filming today."

"How do you know?"

"You kidding? I've been watching those beauties go in there all morning. Let me know if you need any help."

The entrance to Argonaut Productions was guarded by a little guy in a faded security uniform. He was built like a jockey, rail-thin and short. His cap was too big for his narrow skull; it practically rested on his ears. I flashed my badge again and told him I was looking for Auntie Jill.

His head twisted nervously as he spoke. "Ah, I don't know if she's here, I uh . . ."

"Relax, this isn't a raid. There's no problem. Just tell her I want to see her. My name is Nick Polo. Tell her Jack Ryan gave me her name."

He wasn't sure just what to do and ended up leading me down a long, narrow hallway, the walls open, the studs and electrical pipes visible. He showed me into an office and scurried off, almost tripping on his feet in his haste.

The office was a lot better than the hallway: a dark green carpet, white walls lined with shelves and video-cassettes and movie posters. A Danish-modern teak desk was covered with the usual things—papers, staplers, folders. An engraved brass placard sat in one corner of the desk showing the inscription THE FUCK STOPS HERE.

I studied the posters, which showed pictures of well-built men and women in various stages of undress under titles like *Campus Lust*, *Housewives for Hire*, and *Auntie Jill's Fantasies*. *Auntie Jill's Fantasies* must have included the sport of kings. She was all dressed up in leather, brandishing a riding crop.

The rent-a-cop came back puffing his cheeks in and out like he'd just crossed the finish line after the four-hundred-meter.

"Miss Jillian says she'll be with you in a few minutes. Just make yourself at home. Anything you want just ask for, she says. You want to watch them filming?"

"Why not?"

He led me back out to the dingy hallway, the floorboards creaking under our weight, and around to the back half of the building. As we passed through a door, he brought a finger to his lips and motioned me to stand still. He slid open an adjoining door a crack, and after being satisfied that it was all right to enter the magic kingdom, we passed into a high-ceilinged area with a few mock sets—a bedroom, an office, one with a hot tub. A group of ten to twelve people were all huddled together in one brightly lit area. As we got closer, I could see it was a hospital-room set. Two cameramen were checking the lighting around a metal-framed bed, while a guy with casts on his arms and legs lay there, his head twisted to one side, talking to a middle-aged woman in a dark suit.

Across the set was a redhead in a powder blue pantsuit that clung to her classic curves like a layer of cold cream. The hair was shorter and lighter than in the poster, but there was no doubt it was Auntie Jill. She gave me a quick glance, nodded slightly, and went back to her business, which was explaining something to a tall brunette in a nurse's uniform. A makeup man was working on the brunette's face while another guy in faded Levi's and a Hawaiian shirt was doing something to the hem of the uniform.

"Okay, let's go with the scene," shouted Auntie Jill. "Wanda, get him up."

The middle-aged lady in the dark suit nodded, then reached down and grabbed the penis of the guy on the bed. She started stroking it, then bent down and took it in her mouth. Everyone else moved back; the cameramen, neither of which was Oriental, got their cameras ready; another guy swung a boom-mike over the bed. The middle-aged lady pulled her head back, gave the guy's cock an affectionate pat, then walked over to a canvas-backed chair, picked up some knitting needles and a mass of red yarn, and sat down with a smile.

I hadn't paid much attention to the girl in the nurse's uniform before, and she was someone who would be hard not to pay attention to. Her long black hair spilled down to her shoulders. She had the creamy café-au-lait-colored skin that some are lucky enough to be born with and others work for months on the beach trying to obtain. Her eyebrows were thick, her lips full, and when she smiled, she showed large white teeth. It was an animalistic face. The nurse's uniform looked like it was going to burst open any second. Her full breasts pushed against the fabric, her dark nipples easily visible.

"Roll 'em kids, everyone quiet." This from Auntie Jill as she peered over the cameraman's shoulder.

Nursey smiled, approached the bed and said, "I think you need a new prescription." Only it didn't come

53

out quite right. Someone yelled "Cut!" and they started all over again.

It took four tries to get it right, with lots of cursing and laughing between takes. Every time they had to stop for a few minutes, that nice little lady would drop her knitting needles and go and attend to the poor patient's hard-on.

When they finally got what they wanted on film, Auntie Jill announced a lunch break. She walked toward me in a stealthy, padding way, like a cat stalking.

"I'm Jillian Ashbury."

"Nick Polo." We shook hands. "Jack Ryan thought you might be able to help me."

"I owe Jack. Are you a policeman?"

"No. Not anymore."

"In my business, when someone collects on a favor, it's usually one of two things: money or sex. What do you want, Mr. Polo?"

"Just information."

She studied me for a few seconds, nodded, then asked me to follow her. We ended up back in her office.

"What can I do for you?" she asked, settling behind her desk.

I gave her the pictures of Moreno and the girl. "Do you know either of these kids?"

She looked at Moreno first, a frown creasing her forehead. "No, I'd never use him. The tattoos. No good, and he's really not that good-looking. Maybe for an orgy scene, or some kind of biker loop, but no, I don't think I've ever come across him."

The girl was also a negative. "No boobs. If you don't have boobs, either you've got to have a face like Grace Kelly or legs like a fashion model. Even then, it would be tough getting work."

I handed her the pictures with Barbara Martin's head punched out. "What do you think of these? Quality-wise."

She turned on a fluorescent desk lamp and took her time. "Ah, I can see what you're interested in now." She brushed her lower lip with a thumbnail. "The lady with no head is it, isn't she?" Jill looked at me briefly, then went back to the pictures. "She's the focus, the one the cameraman was concentrating on. She reached into a desk drawer and drew out a magnifying glass, the kind with a battery in the handle that lights up the lens. She played it back and forth on the pictures.

"Your lady is no kid, is she? Got to be pushing forty from one side or the other, but in good shape, healthy-looking, not like the two kids."

"Have you ever come across a cameraman, Oriental, probably Filipino, long hair, pockmarked face? Really pockmarked."

"Did he take these?"

"Yes, and a video. The video was well done."

"Umm, that does ring a bell. There was someone like that down in L.A. But I can't think of his name. Is your guy a doper?"

"Yes. Angel dust."

"Yuck." She picked up the phone, punched a button, and asked someone to send Yolanda in. "Angel dust.

He didn't use it himself when he was filming. Not if he wanted things to come out right."

She leaned back in her chair, crossing one long leg over the other. "Is that what they used on your lady? Got her to zombieland, then set those two at her and made pictures, huh?"

"Could be."

"I'll help you all I can. Because I owe Ryan a favor—and because I want to. Your lady was raped. I know how it feels. This business is what I do and I do it well. No one forces me to do the work, and I don't force anyone to do it. I get all kinds of young airheads with great bods and no brains coming in all the time. I send most of them away. It takes a certain kind of person to do porno well. You never heard of anyone going from porno to legitimate films, have you? No, we're typecast. Fuck films. I tell you in a lot of ways it's a lot cleaner than that good old Hollywood cesspool. If I had a dollar for every lap I ran around casting couches in lotusland, I'd be a millionaire. But no matter how fast you run, they catch you one way or the other. You'd need a calculator to add up all the sex scenes I've shot, but I'll tell you something. The one scene I'll always remember was the one when that bastard took me without my permission. So if I can—"

We were interrupted by the brunette in the nurse's uniform, only now she was wearing a short black silky-looking kimono.

"Ah, fresh men," she said as she strode into the office. "Just what we need, Jillian. I'm getting tired of the same old people."

"Yolanda La Mar, meet Nick Polo."

She came over, grabbing my arm, running her hand up to my shoulder. "So nice to meet you," she purred, showing those alligator teeth.

"Back off, Yolanda. He's here on police business."

"So?" Yolanda pouted. "I don't discriminate, baby." Her hand started down my back.

Jillian got out from behind her desk and separated us. "Turn your motor off for a second, dear. Do you remember a cameraman down in L.A. with a heavily pockmarked face? Oriental. Remember him? Didn't he work on the cowboy thing you did a few years back?"

Yolanda pushed out her enormous lips and rolled her eyes. "Yes, he was a strange one, but good with a camera. What was his name? José, that was it!" She clapped her hands together in a loud bang. "Anyway, we called him José." She shouted as though she'd just won first prize on a TV game show. "José Cruz."

"Right, that's it. Thanks Yolanda." Jillian grabbed her by the arm and led her to the door. "Get ready for the next scene; we'll be starting again in a few minutes."

Yolanda gave me an evil smile. "I'm always ready, you know that," she said as she closed the door behind her.

"She seems like a nice, friendly girl," I said.

Jillian gave a sarcastic murmur. "Yolanda just likes it. Men, women, toys. It. She was missing the other day, and I found her next door at the firehouse."

No wonder my fireman friend looked so happy. "Do you remember this Cruz guy?"

"Yes, I do. That was a good six or seven years ago. I don't know if he's even in the business now. He'd done some straight stuff at Fox and M.G.M. The story was, he got kicked out because of drugs. And believe me, to get kicked off a Hollywood lot because of drugs, you've really got to screw up. I think he was from the Philippines. He got into a fight once, came in all bandaged up. They began calling him the Manila Folder. I can ask about him, try and find out if he's around."

"I'd appreciate it, but be careful. This could get rough. Cruz was working with a big guy with a bald head; he's got a Doberman named Satan. Ever hear of him?"

"Never."

I thanked her and gave her my card. I was almost out the door when I remembered another question. "Jill, that nice matronly-looking lady in the blue suit. Who is she? A producer? The film's backer? Or just a horny middle-aged lady who gets tired of knitting all the time."

She steepled her fingers under her chin and smiled up knowingly at me. "She's a fluffer."

Knowing I was nothing more than a straight man, I asked, "Fluffer?"

"Right. It's not easy for the men in this business. The girls can fake everything. But for the guys, well, it's hard being hard at the right times. If we have to take a break in the filming, and we don't want our hero to . . . lose the feeling for the scene, a fluffer comes over and helps him out. You don't want him too excited. Yolanda would wipe him out before we were ready to shoot again. So we use a fluffer. She helps during the dubbing too. We have to redo a lot of the love noises—you know—ummm-mms, ahhhhs, and ooooohs."

I thanked her again and got out of there, suddenly realizing what a sheltered life I'd been leading all these years and wondering how that sweet-looking lady's income tax report looked—Occupation: Fluffer. That should lead to an automatic audit.

7

Walter Peckman was sitting at the bar at Kimball's, swirling a drink in a beefy hand. He drained what was left in the glass in one swallow and ordered a double Jack Daniel's. "Give him whatever he wants, Al," he said to the bartender. I ordered a white wine and, when it came, followed Peckman past the bar, through the restaurant, and over to a corner table. The lunch crowd had left, so the place was fairly deserted.

"Dirty bastards," Peckman said, his voice hoarse, the words slurred. "Dirty bastards. We'll get 'em."

I thought I'd try and cheer him up a little. "I've gotten lucky, Peckman. I've positively identified the boy in the pictures. His name is Richard Moreno. And I'm pretty sure the cameraman is named José Cruz."

"Yeah? Good work. Where are they?"

"That I'm not sure of yet." I gave him a rundown on how I'd identified Moreno and Cruz.

"Real good work, Polo." His voice dropped to a confidential whisper. "But they're shit. Nothing. Hired turkeys. There are three people that gain by Barbara dropping out of the race. Joe Delfino, a fucking farmer from the valley; Dave Grainger, the assemblyman from Eureka; and the Right and Honorable Lawrence Talbot. Now Delfino and Grainger are losers. No way they were ever actually going to get the nomination. But I talked to them all up in Sacramento. I saw all three of the bastards. I let it out that Barbara was thinking of dropping out of the race. Delfino and Grainger almost jumped up and down trying to make a deal, get our backing. But not Talbot. No, Talbot already knew. I've been in this business long enough, pal. He had the look. He knew what I was going to say before the words were out of my mouth. No good bastard."

"Talbot? Lawrence Talbot the senator?"

"State senator. Chicken-shit job. I know. I was one. Shit, the dog catcher has more juice than a state senator. No, he wants the big one. United States senator. Real power. Second best job in the whole damn country. He never had a chance with Barbara in there, so he sets this up." He finished his drink and rattled the cubes at the waiter. "Talbot wouldn't have the guts to do this himself. Too crude. He's got a majordomo. Kostas. Jim Kostas. Goddamn Greek. You know, the only honest Greek I ever met was a statue." He waited until the waiter served his drink. "Cocky dumb bastard. He's the guy, Polo. Get Kostas."

"Get Kostas?"

"Yeah, get him dirty on this. He must think I'm over the hill or something. What the hell did he think I was

61

going to do? Sit back on my ass and let them get away with it? Maybe he thought I'd think that some religious fanatic was behind it all or some crazy that just didn't like the way Barbara combed her hair. No. It's Kostas. And the way to get to Kostas is through Talbot. He's gutless. Scare the shit out of Talbot."

Peckman's confidence seemed to be swelling with each sip of his drink. Mine was sinking down to my socks. "How the hell am I supposed to do all this? Got any ideas?"

"I don't know. That's your job. Just do your job." His eyes narrowed and suddenly he seemed a lot less drunk. "I can give you his office address, a nice cover letter saying you're working for some committee, a letter that'll get you into the capitol, give you a chance to move around, talk to people. Talbot's a pussy. If we can prove that Kostas put those perverts onto Barbara, and that he was working for Talbot, Talbot will fold faster than the poor people's tents after a Republican convention." He smiled at his little joke, then said, "We're going to play hardball with these assholes. Put the pressure on them. I don't care how you do it, spend all the money you need, and I don't care what it costs, just do it."

"Speaking of money."

"You couldn't have spent all the dough I gave you already!"

"I had to pay off a few people to get information. I didn't use just money. I need two boxes of your Cuban cigars."

"Two boxes. Who the hell did you pay off, the Supreme Court?"

We walked back to City Hall. There was a slight drizzle, but it didn't seem to bother Peckman. He was on his hobbyhorse and riding high. We kicked several ideas around and finally decided I'd be a representative of WAPS: Women Against Pornography and Smut. The man from WAPS. Sounded like a corny old spy spoof.

Peckman called the local WAPS office and was treated like royalty. He then made a few calls to Sacramento. This was his ballpark all right, threatening, promising, praising, cursing, maneuvering. He was a master at it. It took him just over an hour and a half to arrange for Mr. George Walker of WAPS to meet with Lawrence Talbot in his office the following morning. I picked the name Walker because I had some phony ID in that name.

We had a bit of an argument about the sudden trip to Sacramento. I wanted to go to Cobb Mountain first and check on Moreno's postal address.

Peckman wasn't buying it. "What does it matter now that we know who the punk is, or who the camera freak is? I'm telling you it was Kostas. I spent a couple of hours with the prick in Sacramento. If it was just the money, I'd listen to you. But this is politics, Polo. And I know politics. Kostas is behind this. Talbot probably doesn't know all the gory details, but he's in on it. You shake him up and nail Kostas. That's the way I want it handled."

All of this freedom was taking a toll on me, so I decided on an early night. Dinner at home, then right to bed.

The telephone jangled me awake. My blurry eyes focused in on the nightstand digital: 1:15 A.M.

"Climax Investigations. We come when you call," I mumbled into the receiver.

There was a throaty laugh. "My, my. Clever line. I'll have to use that in my next movie."

"Why Auntie Jill. What's a nice girl like you doing awake at this time on a working day?"

"I found out a little more about José Cruz. I didn't realize you rough, tough private eyes needed so much beauty sleep."

"I've got to be up early, beat up a couple of gorillas, shoot the guns out of the hands of some Mafia hit men, then tickle the brains out of a few buxom beauties who'll do anything for me as long as I don't tell their husbands about that night on board the aircraft carrier."

The throaty laugh was back. "Wow. You're wasting your time as a detective; screenwriting is your bag. Listen, Cruz was in town a few months ago, did a few loops for my competitors, the Nichols brothers. He still hasn't licked his drug problems. They canned him, don't know where he went. I may be able to run him down though. Why don't we meet tomorrow. If you're not too tired after your busy day, that is. Say dinner?"

"I don't know. I've got to go up north in the morning. Anything on Cruz's partner, the bald guy with the dog?"

"Nope."

"Jill, be careful on this. I'll call you as soon as I get back to town, okay?"

"Okay, sweetheart," she said in one of the worst Bogart impressions I've ever heard, then severed the connection before I had a chance to reply.

8

Sacramento, the state capital, is eighty-eight miles north-east of San Francisco. It is without a doubt the most boring eighty-eight-mile trip I've ever had to make. Over the Bay Bridge, onto Highway 80, then up through long stretches of the industrial areas of the East Bay, then past the oil refineries and empty, colorless hillsides dotted with a few bedroom tracts of homes of the kind they've been building there for the past thirty years. You roll down the car window as you pass by little towns like Pinole and Rodeo, and you wonder how anyone can get used to living with the heavy smell of raw gasoline in the air. When it gets hot in the summer and the winds don't blow for a few days, the odor is so heavy you'd be afraid to light a match.

What happens to their lungs when they go to the mountains and get a whiff of clean air? Do their kids think that's the way air should smell? "What's for dinner tonight, Mom?" "Chicken Chevron, son, and eat your dinner before your soup gets dirty."

There's a more or less mandatory stop about half way between the City and Sacramento, the Nut Tree, a sort of Disneyland of a restaurant with a huge gift shop, rides for the kids, even its own airport. I bought copies of the *Chronicle* and the *Sacramento Bee*, and paged through them over coffee and a waffle. The Martin story was on page 1 in both papers, with pictures of the mayor at her press conference. She looked drawn and tired. I wondered about Peckman's scenario: I somehow get Talbot or Kostas to admit they were the bad boys, turn over all the videos and the pictures and negatives, and then get Talbot to drop out of the upcoming U.S. Senate race. As unlikely as all that was, what about Martin? Was she ever going to bounce back? Not only to politics, but life in general? She'd been raped and brutalized, physically and mentally. I'd seen too many good women who just couldn't handle it for the rest of their lives. Always cringing when touched by their loved ones, crying out when accidentally bumped by a stranger on the street or at the supermarket. Afraid to walk alone, drive alone, but always wanting to sleep alone. I hoped that Martin was one of the strong ones. The ones who made it with the help of family, friends, religion, or just plain old guts.

Sacramento is really a summer town, hot and sticky, graceful old buildings, lots of trees, college campuses, the State Fair, and a couple of pretty rivers that flow through on their way to the delta. The new areas have the usual ticky-tacky homes with air-conditioning and small swimming pools. There are shopping malls every few blocks, fast-food spots opening and closing with dismal regularity, the McDonald's, Wendy's, and Burger Kings fighting for their carcasses and any other open piece of land not yet sacrificed to the greater glory of franchised heartburn. The town somehow looks out of place in bad weather. The rain swells the rivers and turns the flat streets into a blacktop swamp.

Talbot's office was located in a square box of a building a few blocks from the capitol. His secretary was the perky type, in her mid-thirties, hair tied back in a ponytail so tight it made her eyes squint. She had a light freckling across her nose, upon which rested a pair of granny glasses. She gave me an All-American smile. "Can I help you, sir?"

"My name is George Walker. I have an appointment with Senator Talbot."

She checked her calendar, nodded to herself, and turned on the smile again. "He's running just a little late, sir. If you'd just be seated, I'm sure he'll be free in a few minutes."

A few minutes turned out to be fifteen. A man in a dark pin-striped suit, with a curly tangle of dark hair and shoulders like a linebacker, came out of the door I presumed led to Talbot's inner sanctuary, gave me a cold, appraising stare, then said, "Are you Mr. Walker?"

"Right."

"The senator will see you now, but he's got an important meeting coming up, so if you could keep it short, we'd appreciate it."

"Who's we?"

He gave me the glare again, then held out a hand. He was one of those guys that love to intimidate you, if not with a stare, then with one of those bone-crushing handshakes. I moved my hand well up into his so he didn't have any leverage.

"Jim Kostas is my name, Mr. Walker." He turned abruptly to the secretary. "Linda, I'll be back after lunch. Remind the senator of his appointment in about ten minutes, will you?"

He pivoted on his heel and left without waiting for a reply.

"Is he always that cheerful, Linda?"

She smiled over the granny glasses. "This way, sir."

Peckman must have been right about a state senator's clout. I'd seen bigger offices in muffler shops. There was a United States flag and the State of California flag on one wall; another wall covered with the obligatory photographs; a desk, the top empty except for a phone, a blotter, and a lamp; and a few scattered plain wooden chairs.

"How do you do, Mr. Walker? A pleasure to meet you, sir." Talbot extended a hand. Unlike Kostas', it was soft, the fingers long, well manicured. Talbot was one of those guys who could look thirty or fifty, depending on the light and the circumstances. He was well dressed, with graying blondish hair that obviously had been styled and spray-set. He had light gray eyes and the chiseled good looks of a movie star.

He whisked out a chair with the expertise of a headwaiter. "Sit down, sit down, sorry for the rush, you know how it is. Now what can I do for you?"

I opened my briefcase and handed him the photographs of Martin with her head punched out. He examined them quickly.

"Yes, yes, disgusting stuff, Mr. Walker. You and your organization have my sympathy and support; however, the people who make these things wrap themselves in the Constitution, freedom of speech, that sort of thing, but I'm sure you're well aware of that."

"Recognize anyone in those pictures, Senator?"

He took a pair of glasses from his inner suit pocket and looked at the pictures again, tilting them sideways under the desk lamp. "No, certainly not." His voice grew suspicious. "Any reason I should?"

"The boy is named Richard Moreno. I haven't identified the young blond girl. Yet. The lady, now she's someone quite prominent."

"There's certainly no way to tell who she is from these. What exactly is the point of all this, Mr. Walker? Is she someone from my district?"

"The woman was drugged, then raped, and it was all put on film. And in answer to your question, no, she doesn't live in your district, so don't worry about losing a vote."

Talbot upturned a palm. "It's disgusting, sir. But again, why tell me? Surely it's a matter for the police."

"Because you do know her. The pictures were taken at her place in the wine country. St. Helena to be exact. Drugged, raped, and blackmailed. But not for money. For

. . . political reasons. To get her to withdraw from an upcoming election."

Talbot stared at me for a good twenty seconds. The blood was slowly draining from his face. "Are you trying to tell me—"

"I'm not trying, Talbot. I'm saying someone played a rotten trick on that lady, and I'm going to fix it for her, one way or the other."

He burst from his chair, bumping clumsily into the desk as he came toward me. "Just who the hell are you? You can't come in here and accuse me of blackmailing Ba—"

"No names. She's suffered enough. So let's keep her name out of it."

"This is the most ridiculous thing I've ever heard of," he said, walking back to his desk and sitting down. "It's just preposterous."

Talbot was shook, no doubt about it. Even though he was a politician, he couldn't be that good an actor. "I guess you're the favorite to become the party nominee for the U.S. Senate now, aren't you?"

He picked up the phone, thought better of it, and slammed the receiver back on its cradle.

"There was another guy at the picture party. Big man, bald head, had a Doberman named Satan. That ring any bells, Talbot?"

"Don't be absurd. I would never get involved in anything like this." He was looking right at me, but his eyes weren't focusing. "I'll keep these and get back to you as soon as possible. You can—"

"No way." I reached over and grabbed his forearm. He started to resist, then dropped the pictures to the desk. "I want it all, Talbot. The pictures, the negatives, the names of everyone involved. Your friends can keep the thirty thousand dollars. But I want everything else. Then I want your ass."

"Surely you can't be serious. I tell you—"

"No. I tell you. You're in shit. You've got a reputation I'm sure you want to keep. There must be something other than politics that would interest a gentleman like yourself."

He pulled in his chin and his face wrinkled like a fan. The reality of it started to sink in. He leaned back, and the chair creaked like elderly arthritic joints.

"You're not to contact the lady in the photograph. She doesn't know of your involvement, and if you play ball with me, she never will. Now I know you've got an important engagement. Keep it. I'll be back here at two o'clock. By then you should be able to give me the information I need."

I left him sitting in a dazed state.

Linda was pounding away at her typewriter. I gave her my best smile. "Nice guy, Senator Talbot. Too bad he's on such a tight schedule." I glanced at my wrist watch. "He suggested I talk to Mr. Kostas, but I have another appointment right now. Do you know where Kostas is having lunch?"

"He usually eats at the Firehouse, Mr. Walker."

The Firehouse was a class operation in the Old Sacramento Historic District. I used a pay phone in the lobby and called the restaurant, verifying the fact that Kostas had a luncheon reservation for eleven forty-five.

I went back by Talbot's office and waited twenty minutes, but neither he came out, nor did Kostas go in. I went back to the phone and checked the list of confidential sources, as we say in the PI business. Kostas wasn't listed in the phone book.

I called Walter Peckman's office, but he wasn't in and his secretary didn't know when he was expected. I tried Peckman's home number, got his answering machine, and left a short message that I had met with Talbot and had lit a fire under his behind. The County Administration Building was only a few blocks away, so I decided to try and run down a local address for Kostas and Talbot. Neither was listed in voter registration records, which wasn't surprising. Talbot would have to vote in his own district, and Kostas would want to—every vote counted. The assessor files showed James D. Kostas at 1445 Madison Avenue. Nothing for Talbot. I killed a little more time digging through civil records, but nothing came up. It was getting close to Kostas' lunch time, so I drove over to the Firehouse.

The Historic District is just that, a part of Sacramento dating back to the Gold Rush days. They had done a good job reconstructing and sprucing up the old wood-framed buildings, filling them with an assortment of restaurants, gift shops, novelty stores, and museums.

I was sitting at the Firehouse's bar when Kostas walked in. He was with two gentlemen, both middle-aged, expensively tailored. I called to him as he passed by. He gave me a vague look, trying to categorize me. I grabbed his hand, caught the pressure point I wanted, and squeezed hard. "You remember me, Jim. I was in Talbot's office this morning."

His two luncheon companions were staring at us.

"I guess you haven't spoken to Talbot, huh, Jim?" I said, releasing his hand with a final jerk.

"What was your name again, friend?"

"Walker. If I were you, I'd give Talbot a call right away."

Kostas turned and invited his guests to go to their table. "I'll be right with you, fellas." He waited until they were out of earshot, then turned back to me. "Now what's this about me calling the senator?"

"He's been trying to get ahold of you, Jim. Real hard."

"How the hell would you know? What was your meeting all about?"

"Your friend. The bald guy with the dog. Satan." I patted his cheek. "You're a bad boy, Jimmy."

Until then I was just taking shots in the dark, muddying up the waters, really not quite believing Peckman's conclusions about Talbot and Kostas. But I struck a bullseye when I mentioned Old Baldy and Satan to Kostas. He rocked back on his heels as if he'd been struck, then took a deep breath, like a diver getting ready to go to the bottom. The bartender was giving us a funny look.

"Don't ever touch me like that again, buddy."

"Oh, you don't like being touched? How do you

think she felt, Jimmy? You set her up first, didn't you? You had the date with her, called her, canceled, then sent your—"

He reached back with his right hand before throwing the punch, which gave me plenty of time to step inside and block it with my left arm. I ground my heels into the carpet and swiveled in, throwing my right elbow into his stomach. The elbow is a wonderful thing. Nice to have for leaning on bars, or flicking on the light switch when your hands are full. But when you use it as a weapon, it can do a lot of damage. It's small, hard, relatively pointed at the end. The tip of my elbow punctured Kostas' stomach muscles, and his breath whooshed out like air from a punctured tire. I backed away and let him slowly sink to his knees. I slapped a twenty on the bar. "Fix Mr. Kostas and his friends a drink. I think they'll need it."

Not too shabby for an exit line, huh? I got the Granada and maneuvered it around to a spot where I could watch the front of the restaurant.

Ten minutes later Kostas stalked out, handed a ticket to the parking attendant, and waited, making a catcher's mitt of one hand and a baseball with the other, pounding them together with increasing anger.

He was in his car, a silver Thunderbird, almost before the attendant got out from behind the wheel. The rain had started up, and the car's tires squealed as it took off. The heavy traffic kept Kostas from getting very far ahead of me, so it was no problem to follow him right back to the parking lot next to Talbot's office. Since I had a little time before my scheduled meeting with Talbot, I had a few choices: go to a movie, a museum, a bar, or check out Kostas' place.

The rain had let up a bit. I jumped out of the car and ran over to Kostas' T-bird, bent down as if tying my shoe, and used my pocketknife to puncture first the left rear, then the left front, tire.

I stopped off at a Standard station and had the tank topped off. Now I know we can blame the Arabs for the price of gas, and for forcing the stations to stop frills, like checking the oil and water and that kind of thing, but charging a dollar for a map of Sacramento? Give us a break, oh Mighty Moguls.

Kostas' place was off Highway 80, a huge two-hundred-plus-unit apartment complex that had been turned into condominiums, called Shelter Creek. A cement-bottomed ditch about two inches deep filled with murky water wandered through the area. There was a large wooden billboard map showing where the individual apartments were located. Kostas' was in unit C6, which was right by the community swimming pool.

I rang his bell several times, waited a couple of minutes, then tried to slip the door with a few old plastic-coated bank calendars I always kept in my wallet. The calendars are good. A piece of nice solid celluloid with the edges sanded down is better, but they're hard to find nowadays. Whatever you do, never try to use a credit card like they do on TV. We had a string of hot-prowl rapes. The guy was slick: loided the front or back door, raped the occupant, then stole anything of value. He was a meticulous bastard, never left a print; the poor victims always had their eyes blindfolded with a towel, or a pillowcase, or their clothing. The hot merchandise never turned up. We caught him because the credit card he used broke off, leaving the part with his name right inside the door. He MasterCarded himself right into San Quentin.

Kostas' door was tight with weather stripping, so the calendars wouldn't slide into the jam. I walked around to the rear of the building. The ground sloped away, making it a good ten-foot climb to his back porch. I went back to the car, drove a few blocks, found a K-Mart, and went shopping for burglar tools: a small crowbar, the type carpenters use to pull nails; a pair of thin work gloves; and a kitchen spatula. The next stop was at a supermarket for a few rolls of toilet paper and napkins, just enough to fill up a shopping bag, and a newspaper.

There was no sign of Kostas, or his car, back at his apartment. I rang the bell again, waited, then, using the shopping bag as a shield, went to work on the door. I kept my eyes on the apartment next door as I slowly pried the bar into the jam. I had to pound and push like hell but finally wiggled it in a good half inch. I pushed some more, then slid the spatula down toward the bolt. There was a loud cracking noise as the door gave way. I stood motionless, waiting for the neighbors to jump out at me or an alarm to go off. Nothing. I opened the door, reached in, undid the handle lock, twisted it a couple of times to make sure it worked, then closed the door again, stuffing the rolled-up newspaper between the knob and the jam. It covered up the damaged wood pretty well. I hotfooted it back to my car, drove a block, parked, and waited. I gave it a good fifteen minutes, the motor on, the windshield wipers beating a steady tattoo, clearing the rain. Sacramento's finest should have made an appearance by now if there had been a silent alarm. I dropped the crowbar and spatula down a sewer gutter and made my way back to Kostas' place.

It was a two-bedroom affair, with a small L-shaped living and dining room. A sliding glass door opened onto a sun deck containing two folded-up lounge chairs and a gas barbecue covered with plastic. Burglar's rule number one: always have a second exit. Even if it meant a ten-foot drop onto concrete.

The living-dining room had that sparse-chilly look of a place where nobody actually lived. The walls were a dull green, and the furniture consisted of a black naugahide couch, a matching chair, and a dusty coffee table littered with old magazines: *People, Sunset, TV Guide.* One bedroom was small, neat, just a single bed covered with a green corduroy spread and a walnut dresser.

The other bedroom was large, with an unmade king-sized bed, the sheets looking like they were in need of an oil change. The floor was strewn with mismatched pairs of shoes, shirts, pants, underwear. A walnut dresser, a match for the one in the other room, had two of its drawers partially opened. I checked through the drawers, found the usual array of shorts, undershirts, socks, and pulled them out and dumped them all on the floor. The end tables alongside the bed were more revealing. Some silk undies, male and female, two pink battery-operated vibrators, one the size of a small baseball bat, a tube of an apricot-colored gel labeled Dr. Jay's Joy Juice, and a pearl-handled .45 automatic. I dumped everything onto the floor except the gun. It was loaded, one round in the chamber, ready to go. I ejected it, then slipped the rounds one by one from the magazine like lozenges.

I checked the bathroom. The toilet tank top was covered with magazines: *Playboy*, *Penthouse*, *Hustler*. The sink was smeared with drops of toothpaste and dark hair bristles. The medicine cabinet was jammed with the usual stuff: shaving soaps, deodorants, and aspirin. I dropped the .45 into the toilet bowl.

The view from the bedroom window was sliced into pencil gray lines by a set of Venetian blinds. The swimming pool was being prickled by the slow, steady rain. I checked my watch. I'd been in the apartment six minutes. A closet covered one wall. A dozen suits and sport coats were packed in with a few very sexy-looking dresses. One dress was size six, the other two were tens. Kostas' suit jacket was a forty-six, so I could forget any ideas I had about him being a cross-dresser. Apparently some of his lady friends had left their gowns behind, or maybe he collected them as souvenirs. I reached in and began tossing everything on the floor. There was a shelf above the suit-rack filled with shoes and hats. One thing caught my eye—a photo album. There were pictures of Kostas as a young man in a football uniform, some shots of him in the army, then a parade of attractive young girls. I dropped them on the floor with the clothes.

The kitchen probably would have been described by a realtor as being compact: stove, refrigerator, sink, and a gray Formica table and two chairs. The refrigerator was almost bare, the cupboards stocked with a minimum of mismatched plates, cups, and glasses. The only thing that looked like it got any regular work was the Mr. Coffee machine.

There was a clutter of mail, some opened, some not, on the table, along with a telephone-answering machine. I thumbed through the mail—lots of bills, several party invitations from corporations on thick, heavy bond paper. Nothing personal. No written notes, no appointment book, just a calendar from a lumber supply company hanging next to the yellow wall phone. There were a few unintelligible scribblings on the calendar dates. I checked for the day Barbara Martin was attacked. It was blank.

The message counter on the answering machine was up to eight-four, so I rewound the tape and pushed the play button. The first call was from a female voice I recognized—Talbot's secretary—asking Kostas to call the office immediately. There were two calls where no message was left, then a call from a man. The words: "It's Bill. A little trouble. Nothing I can't handle. We better talk." A chill ran right up my back and worked its way through the shoulders. There was no mistaking that voice. The man who called Peckman's office. The same voice that told me where to take the money. There were two more calls with no messages, probably Talbot's secretary again. I rewound the tape and replayed it. Bill. So now I at least had a name for him. I pried up the top of the machine. There were two tapes, one for incoming and one for outgoing calls. I pocketed the incoming tape, then decided to take both of them, figuring I might as well make Kostas as mad as possible. I went back to his mail, found the latest phone bill, and slipped that into the pocket with the tapes.

My hands were sweating inside the cheap cotton gloves as I opened the front door, half expecting to see Kostas and the Sacramento Police Department Tac Squad waiting for me. There was nothing but the rain.

9

Talbot's secretary had lost some of her perkiness. She looked at me suspiciously over her granny glasses. "Senator Talbot is out. I'm not sure when he'll be in."

"I had an appointment."

"Several people had appointments," she said irritably.

"How about Mr. Kostas? Is he in?"

"No, he's not. And I have the feeling that you are the reason both of them are nowhere to be found. They asked me if you had left a card. I called the offices of Women Against Pornography and Smut, Mr. Walker. They never heard of you."

"You must have called the wrong branch."

"Which branch do you work out of?"

"The one you didn't call," I said, backing out the door. "Tell Talbot and Kostas I'll be in touch."

I tried getting ahold of Peckman again, but he was still unavailable, which left me the choice of hanging around Sacramento and harassing Kostas and Talbot some more, or going back to San Francisco and dining with a porno star. I dialed Jill Ashbury's number; she was in, and available. Dinner was arranged for eight o'clock at the Iron Horse.

On the drive back to the City, I tried to figure out my next move. Kostas and Talbot were probably butting heads right now, so what I did depended a lot on just what they came up with. How would they react? Hang tough? Stonewall? Just deny everything? That was probably the smart thing to do. The dumb thing to do was confront them like I did. But Peckman had called the shot. "We're going to play hardball with these assholes," he said. Well, I hope he was ready for a few line drives back his way. Could he handle them? Could Barbara Martin? It would have been nice if I'd been able to hire a couple of operatives to follow Kostas and Talbot around. Especially Kostas. He'd be a raging bull when he got back to his apartment. I wasn't kidding myself. I'd caught him with a lucky punch in the bar. I didn't relish tangling with him again, when he had time to think and room to maneuver those big shoulders. He had the look of a man who didn't like losing. Especially in public.

I patted the tapes in my pocket. Good old Bill. Was he the big bald guy? Who else? I mentally kicked myself for not having set up a recorder on Peckman's office line.

When I got back to my flat, the first thing I did was stash the tapes in the compartment behind the kitchen sink; then I went over Kostas' phone bill, dialing each number and asking for Bill. The calls were all over the state: Los Angeles, Orange County, Eureka; a half dozen to San Francisco that turned out to be attorneys' offices and the local Democratic headquarters; dozens in Sacramento. There were a few Bills, but not the right one.

No calls to Martin's place in St. Helena, or to her office. And none to Cobb Mountain, where Richard Moreno had a postal box. The bills were for last month, way before the St. Helena mess. I'd love to get a look at his latest billing. But would Kostas make calls from his house that could be traced?

I was in the middle of shaving when the phone rang. It was Inspector Jack Ryan.

"Hey, Polo. Remember those pictures you showed me? The guy with the mug shot and the little blond thing?"

"Yeah, what about them?"

"I think the girl is dead. Bob Tehaney from Homocide came over, showed me a new victim. Thought I might know her from a vice scam."

"You sure it was her?"

"No, but the odds would have to be pretty heavy for me to bet against it."

"Did you get her name?"

"Debbie something. Debbie Bishop."

"How and where?"

"Knife. Very professional job, according to Tehaney. They found the body dumped in Golden Gate Park. No idea where she was actually killed."

"Did you mention anything about me to Tehaney?"

There was a long pause. "No, I thought I'd let you handle that."

"Thanks, Jack. I will. See you later. I've got a dinner date with Jill Ashbury and I'm running late."

"You do move in interesting circles, Nick. Be careful."

I put the telephone back gently on its cradle and stared at it stupidly. There was shaving cream on one side of the mouthpiece.

The Iron Horse was filled. There was a good smell to the place, the hum of conversation and the serious sound of glasses tinkling, of corks being pulled, of knives and forks on dinnerware. Jill Ashbury sat waiting in one of the red leather booths. She was wearing a lettuce green silk dress cut low in the front. A silver ice bucket holding a sweating bottle of champagne stood alongside the table.

Victor, the maître d', smiled knowingly when I mentioned I was dining with Miss Ashbury.

"I thought you might be a no-show," she said as I slid into the booth.

"I don't think you'd have been lonely for long. Not in that outfit." Her hair was swept back, accenting her delicate features.

Dinner went well. What the hell, it was Peckman's expense money. Escargots, Caesar salad, scallops sauté, and cheesecake. All washed down with two bottles of Roeder's Cristal champagne.

"Why Auntie Jill, what big teeth you have," I said, draining the last sip of wine as she finished her dessert. "How do you keep your girlish figure tucking it away like that?"

"Thanks for the compliment. I think. The secret is

84

to eat like this just once a week. Besides, it's your treat."
She paused. "But I think I can pay for my supper in another way. I've found José Cruz for you."

"How?"

"Actually Yolanda found him. She was at a party last night and ran into someone who worked with him recently. He was fired off his last picture. Too bad, really. Drugs again. Apparently he picked up the habit in Vietnam. He was good with a camera, all right. That's what he did in the war."

"For who? Television?"

"No. The army. They had their own camera crews. Anyway, he was living in Berkeley. The address is 762 Haste."

"Where's Yolanda now?"

"I don't know. She thought she might be able to find out some more about José for you. She's taken a liking to you, Nick. 'Such a nice, fresh man.'"

"Jill, try and find out where she is. Call her. Tell her to forget it. Remember those pictures I showed you? The boy with the tattoos and the blond girl? Well, the girl was found in Golden Gate Park. Murdered."

Her green eyes widened. "Do you think it had something to do with . . . the woman in your pictures?"

"I'd bet on it. And I'd feel a lot safer if Yolanda was home in bed with the First Armored Division, rather than out asking questions."

"I'll see what I can do," she said, wiggling from the booth. Victor steered her to the telephone, and I watched the male diners get tennis neck as they followed her progress.

She was back in fifteen minutes. "No luck. I tried every place I could think of."

"Where's she staying?"

"In one of the units in my apartment house. I own the building."

"The Shadow was wrong. Crime does pay. Are you sure about that address in Berkeley?"

"Yes, I'm good at remembering numbers."

"Let's go for a ride."

10

Every time I drive into Berkeley I feel like I should have my passport stamped. Years ago it was a nice, fairly quiet village surrounding the radical campus of the University of California. Lately Cal has turned somewhat conservative and the good mothers and fathers of Berkeley have turned slightly to the left of Fidel Castro.

The main drag is University Avenue, a boulevard sprinkled with a couple of very good restaurants, dozens of bad ones, and all the hookers they keep kicking out of Oakland.

The city planners came up with an idea to keep traffic off the side streets and onto University. Little concrete barriers greet you at almost every intersection, so you find yourself driving around in circles a lot.

Seven sixty-two Haste was a shingled old Victorian that even in the dark looked like it was badly in need of repairs.

"Lock the doors, keep the motor running, and at the first sign of trouble, beep the horn like crazy," I told Jill.

She shivered. "You don't think Yolanda is in there, do you?"

"No, but José Cruz may be." I reached around her back and she slid over, mistaking my intentions. I punched in the backrest and took out the .38 revolver and handed it to her. "Have you ever used one of these before?"

"Yes."

"Good. If I'm not back in five minutes, start beeping that horn."

A picket fence like a row of bad teeth bordered the front of the house. The rain had stopped, but a cold wind whistled through the willow tree that bumped up against the front steps. From somewhere in the back of the building came the sound of someone playing Chopin on an out-of-tune piano. There were several rusty mailboxes nailed to the wall next to the front door. J. CRUZ was scribbled on a piece of white paper and Scotch-taped to the box labeled APT. B. The front door wasn't locked. The hallway retained some of the splendor of the original house: faded and chipped marble floor; high beamed ceiling, the beams thick; and even through layers of dust, the quality of the mahogany shone through. There was a large sitting room off to the right, filled with old stuffed furniture from a different era and dozens of potted cactus plants.

I took the stairway and hurried to the second floor. A bright brass letter *B* stood out against the washed-out gray paint of the first door at the top of the landing. I knocked, then stood to one side, my hand cradling the Beretta in my pants pocket. No response. I tapped again. Still nothing, just the tinkling of the piano from downstairs. I tried the plastic calendars again, and this time they slid the lock easily. The room was no more than ten by ten. A bed, a bare mattress spotted with rust-colored stains, a cheap knotty pine dresser, and a table the size of a typing stand. The closet door was opened showing a few metal hangers and dust balls on the floor. I trooped back outside just as Jill was starting to blow the horn. She stopped when she saw my arms flapping.

"Looks like our boy flew the coop," I said as she rolled down the window. "I'm going to try and find the manager, see what he knows."

"You're not leaving me alone any longer, Polo," she said, sliding across the car seat.

"You can help. We'll be film producers, looking for Cruz, got a hot job for him, that kind of thing. Think you can handle it?"

She slammed the door, shoved the .38 down the front of my waistband, and glared at me as she wrapped a white feather boa around her shoulders. "Handle it? I've done some acting in my time, buster, and it wasn't all from the prone position."

We found the piano player in the rear portion of the house. He was a scholarly-looking man with long white hair and a large condor nose. He was dressed in a formal-looking black suit and had gone from Chopin to Gershwin's "The Man I Love."

"Excuse me," Jill said. "Are you the manager?"

He looked at us, his long bony fingers still pressing

89

the piano keys, but not hard enough to make a sound. "What can I do for you?"

Jill went over, leaned against the piano, and bent over slightly. "I'm trying to find José Cruz. We're doing a film and I need him badly. José is such a talented cameraman, but he's so difficult to get ahold of. You know how artists are, don't you?"

The old man stood up, bowed courtly, and kissed her hand. "Certainly. I'm Roland Wilson, the owner of this property. José Cruz. Yes. Apartment B. He moved about six days ago, didn't leave a forwarding address, I'm afraid."

"Did Cruz have many visitors? A young Latin boy around twenty, or a blond girl about the same age?"

He reluctantly took his eyes off Jill to answer me. "No, no one like that that I know of. Of course, I don't spy on my guests. Unless they do something disagreeable."

He turned his attention back to Jill. "He seemed a nice man, kept to himself. No problem, just that one time."

"Which time was that?" Jill asked sweetly.

"The dog. Monster of a dog. I like animals, but really. Big dog, small man, I always say. One of his visitors came with this black brute. I had to warn him. No animals allowed."

"The dog. Was it a Doberman?" I asked.

"Yes. They always remind me of Nazis, storm troopers, that kind of thing."

"Did you get a look at the man? The man with the dog?"

He took a deep breath, pursing his narrow, wrinkled lips. "A disagreeable-looking chap. Very big. Bald. He didn't like it when I told him the dog had to go outside. Didn't like it at all. But one has to be firm about those kinds of things."

"Do you remember when he was here?"

"The day before Mr. Cruz moved out, I believe."

There was some scratch paper by a telephone perched on the top of the piano. I wrote down my name and phone number. "It really is important for us to contact Cruz. If you hear anything, or if he happens to get any mail, would you call us?"

He stared at the address, and I could see he wasn't going to go for it.

"It would be most . . ."

"It would be most wonderful if you could do that," Jill interrupted. She moved close to him. "I'd be so appreciative."

He took her hand and kissed it again. "It would be my pleasure. You know, if you don't mind my saying so, you look very familiar, young lady. Do you play?"

Jill raised both eyebrows.

"The piano. I used to, before these betrayed me," he said, waving his arthritic fingers. "Now I just teach."

I said, "Did you happen to hear Cruz call the bald man by his name? Or see what kind of car he was driving?"

"No. The only name I heard was the dog's. Satan. It seemed appropriate."

"Nice old guy," I said when we were back in the car and headed toward the Bay Bridge.

91

"He may never play a concert again with those fingers, but he still knows how to pinch a fanny with them. Was I helpful?"

"He never would have opened up that much to me," I admitted.

"What'll you do next?"

"I'm not sure. First I'd like to make sure that Yolanda is okay."

Jill's apartment building was out on Potrero Hill, a neighborhood that was originally Russian and Irish, then black. Now the yuppies and real estate promoters were moving in and taking advantage of the views and, for San Francisco, fairly reasonable prices.

I parked in front of Jill's garage door. It was an eight-unit place—stucco, and aluminum windows. She stopped at apartment number 4. Bossa nova music was coming from a radio or phonograph. Jill knocked and Yolanda came to the door, her black hair a tangled mess of snakes, piled high on her head. The pupils of her dark eyes were wide with excitement. She was wearing skin-tight yellow spandex pants and a white tube top.

"Ah, come join the party."

"Not tonight," said Jill. "Did you find out anything more about José Cruz?"

Her full lips pouted. "No, nothing."

"I'll talk to you in the morning," Jill said.

Someone called to Yolanda over the music and she smiled, gave me a wink, and closed the door.

"Doesn't her motor ever wear down?"

"It hasn't yet," Jill said. "I'm afraid she's just going to come to a complete stop one of these days."

Jill's apartment was actually two units converted into one. The furniture was Danish modern—lots of teak and leather. A picture window gave a sparkling view of the South Bay.

"What can I fix you?" she asked.

"I think I better get going, Jill. It's been a long day."

"Oh, really." Her head tilted to one side as she studied me. "Well, I think my bravo acting performance deserves at least one drink for celebration." She walked to a wall bar and selected some crystal snifters and a bottle of Rémy Martin from a mirrored shelf.

"When," I said as the cognac got near the top of the glass.

"Cheers, private eye." She took a healthy swallow, then perched on the edge of a white leather sofa.

I sipped at my drink, looking at her. Gorgeous, sexy. A walking wet dream for legions of middle-aged men in raincoats and pimply-faced kids sitting in dark theaters with jackets over their laps. And bright. And witty, and, judging from the looks of the apartment house, smart with a dollar. And available. Then why was I feeling like a sophomore at the prom who wanted nothing more than a kiss on the cheek and a handshake?"

"Sit down, Nick," she said, patting the cushions beside her. "I've been doing a little private investigation on my own. Nick Polo. Ex-cop, ex-husband, and now ex-con."

"My, my. You have been doing some checking, haven't you?" I sat down at the far end of the couch.

"A little. You were working for an attorney. His client was involved in some kind of a drug deal. Got killed by some junkie or another dealer, and you found all this money, right?"

"Something like that."

"Something like a half million dollars in cash. Good, clean, negotiable cash." She stretched lazily. "So you and the attorney decided, what the hell, it was just money—who knows who it actually belonged to?—so you decided to split it between the two of you."

"It seemed like a good idea at the time."

She swilled the brandy around in the glass, watching it cling to the side. "But he got cold feet, turned his portion of the money over to the feds. And dumped on you."

"Sad story, isn't it? Think you can sell the screen rights?"

She moved in closer to me. "Tell me, Nick. Really. How was it in prison?"

"Different."

"What about . . . what about the homosexuals? Did they bother you?"

"I wore a T-shirt that said I Cured AIDS Through Self-hypnosis. Nobody bothered me."

She chuckled and reached over and undid my tie. "I bother you a little bit though, don't I? What is it? That Catholic upbringing of yours?" Her hands worked behind the tie and starting undoing my shirt buttons. "Or are you just a little holier than thou? Is that it, Nick? I'm a scarlet woman and not good enough for you? A little reverse on the old double standard." She put her drink down and used both hands on the shirt, her fingernails raking lightly over my chest, her hair burrowing into my chin as she started kissing her way down farther as each button came undone. She stopped as she got to my belt buckle and looked up at me with mocking eyes. "Is that what's bothering you, baby?"

"No," I croaked. "All I'm worried about is whether or not you've got a fluffer hidden in one of the closets."

11

"He's humming, can you beat that, the son of a bitch is humming," said Lieutenant Bob Tehaney, a toothpick lingering forgotten in the corner of his mouth.

We were outside the coroner's lab, looking through the window as an autopsy was being performed on Debbie Bishop.

"How the hell can a guy do that kind of work and hum? I wonder what the hell the tune is?"

"Beats me, Bob." Tehaney was an old-timer, with over thirty-five years on the job, a tall, thin, sandy-haired man who only took one thing in life seriously: the Notre Dame football team. One of his sons was a pretty good athlete and had been recruited by several colleges, Notre Dame among them. Bob couldn't believe it when the boy decided to go to USC. "But what about the Notre Dame campus?" Bob had asked him. "What about the tradition?" The kid, a true Californian, told him that both the campus and the tradition were covered with four feet of snow.

Tehaney kept his eye on the coroner. "What the hell's your action in this, Nick?"

"I'm looking for a missing kid. She looks quite a lot like this victim, Bob. Irish girl from Boston," I added. "Her name was Bishop too. Jane Bishop."

"You saying they're related?"

"No. My clients say their girl was an only child. A coincidence, I guess."

"I don't trust coincidences." He swiveled to look at me. "Do you?"

"Nope."

"This poor girl was from Texas. Nineteen years of age. I spoke to her parents. Farmers. She left home a couple of years ago. They'd get a postcard from her now and then. That was it." He ran a freckled hand through his hair. "Kids, they're a wonder, aren't they? The parents didn't even know she was in San Francisco. She looked pretty beat up for her years. Track marks on her arms, back of her poor legs. Bruises all over her body."

"Any idea where she was killed?"

"Not yet. And no weapon either. It was a damn sharp knife. Cut her ear from ear. Almost surgical."

"Where was she living?"

"Don't know. She didn't have an ID on her. We just got lucky on her prints. She'd been busted a few times. Prostitution."

"Here in the City?"

97

Tehaney rubbed his chin. "Why all the interest, Nick."

"Just curious. Like I said, strange coincidence, the name, both nineteen. What was her date of birth?"

"August the fourth. And your Miss Bishop. What was her date of birth?"

"March seventeenth."

"Hmmmmph," Tehaney snorted. "An Irish girl from Boston born on St. Patrick's Day. How about that? Strange world, isn't it, Bucko. Full of coincidences. Like you getting out of jail just a couple of days ago and already working on a case. From Boston. Wouldn't think you'd have time to get your feet wet that quickly, now would you?" He turned back to the autopsy room. The examination was completed and the coroner was pulling off his gloves. "Damn heathen. He's still humming a tune. I hope it's not 'Danny Boy.' Keep in touch, Nick. In case any more coincidences come up."

I used a pay phone at a service station and tried Peckman again. He was still away from his office, and his secretary had no idea when he'd be back. His home number was answered by a recorded message, Peckman's voice advising that he was out and to leave a message at the beep.

I went home and checked my own answering machine. No calls.

Now this is illegal, and I know you'd never try it, and anyway, it doesn't work all the time. Automatic answering machines, especially the cheaper models that can be operated by a remote call, all work on the same principle. One tone, or a combination of tones, activate the machine so you can call your own number from wherever, punch a combination of the numbers on a touch-tone telephone, and the machine plays back all your messages for you. There are only so many tones, so if you just keep pressing the buttons long enough, you're just liable to hit the right ones.

I dialed Peckman's number again, waited for the ever-popular beep, then started playing musical notes on the buttons. It took a couple of minutes, then there was the sound of the tape rewinding. The first two calls were familiar: my voice asking Peckman to get ahold of me. The next voice was familiar also: Jim Kostas sounding pissed off as hell. "Okay, we'll meet. The time and place are okay. But I'm not going to put up with anymore of this harassment shit. I mean it."

There were a few dry spots where people had called without leaving a message, then my own sweet voice again. Kostas' call was sandwiched in between my messages, meaning he had called sometime between noon and 7 P.M. yesterday. What was Peckman up to? Kostas and Talbot wouldn't have to be geniuses to figure out who I was working for. They must have called Peckman and screamed bloody murder. So Peckman had arranged some kind of a meeting. I broke open a box of the Cuban cigars, the one I hadn't delivered to Harry Saito, used a steak knife to nip off the end of one, and lit up. Addictive damn things. Well, Holmes had his cocaine, Kojak his lollypops, and Travis McGee his houseboat and suntan. We all need a crutch. I paced up and down, puffing away, trying to figure out what the hell to do next. The right thing to do was drop it all in Bob Tehaney's lap. Tell him about poor little Debbie Bishop's connection to Richard Moreno and José Cruz and let the immortal wheels of justice grind into action.

I had no way of running Cruz down the easy way, through Motor Vehicles. Not without a date of birth; it was just too common a name. You want to disappear in today's modern, technological world? No problem. Just pick a name like Jim Smith, Jack Jones, or José Cruz. Keep your date of birth off public records like voter registration files and credit reports. Pay cash for everything, and move around every once in a while. You're as good as invisible. I could run a check on Debbie Bishop now that I had her date of birth. Maybe some of her arrests were local and addresses could be developed, something to tie her to Moreno or Cruz, but I didn't want to risk Tehaney getting ahold of it. He'd given me the benefit of the doubt for now, but if I stuck my nose into his case again, I'd better come up with some answers. So that left me waiting for Peckman to call or acting on the one slim lead I did have. Moreno's postal box in Cobb Mountain.

12

"Gee, I don't know if I should do this."

I gave her what I hoped was my most winning smile.
"It's the federal law, young lady. That subpoena I gave
you is for Mr. Richard Moreno." I gave her the same line
I had given the postal clerk in San Francisco. "If you
don't give us his correct address, we'll have to subpoena
you and you can explain things to the judge."

The girl was in her mid-twenties, dressed in faded
khakis and a heavy green plaid shirt, rather than the typical gray postal uniform. She examined the phony subpoena again, nodded, and went to the phone. The
cautious type. The Cobb Mountain Post Office was a one-
room cubicle in downtown Cobb. Downtown consisting of
a coffee shop, a real estate office, and a hardware store.
The parking lot was full of pickup trucks, mostly the four-
wheel-drive variety with rifle racks on the back window.

She hung up with an apologetic grin on her face.
"Sorry, but I thought I'd better check with the super-

visor." She handed me a piece of yellow paper. "That's the address we have for Mr. Moreno. It's a cabin on the old Rothman Resort property."

I remembered Rothman's. It was a very popular family resort during the fifties: cabins, swimming pool, fishing, golf, big dances on weekends, mineral spring baths. It had died out when they opened the freeways leading to Lake Tahoe and people found that they could go up to Tahoe and gamble, or even fly to Hawaii for what a week at Rothman's cost.

"I'd better draw you a map," she said, taking back the paper. "You go left there on Bottlerock Road, you'll pass the place where the swimming pool was, turn left and go about a half mile. Mr. Moreno was in not too long ago to check his box. He never seems to get much mail. Just a letter once a month or so. Some kind of check, I guess."

I thanked her and went out to the car. A cup of coffee and a sandwich would have hit the spot, but I'd just as soon see as few locals as possible now that the girl had verified that Moreno was in the area.

I drove along the route she suggested. There was a fairly large motel and a lot of new cabin construction. I remembered reading an article about the area beginning to boom again because they were opening the mountains for thermoenergy. You could smell the sulphur in the air.

The former Rothman's swimming pool was a half-filled hole now. Someone had dumped some dirt in there and was planting something. Something that looked like it died last summer. I turned left onto a dirt road and drove past a few deserted cabins, the doors and windows boarded over, the redwood planking ripped from the sun decks. The area was thick with pine trees; some looked to be over sixty feet high, swaying in a chilly wind.

The road got worse the farther I got in, and I had to skirt around several large chuckholes filled with water. No wonder there were so many four-wheel-drive trucks around. I kept an eye on the odometer and was just past a half mile when I saw a large, ramshackle cabin with smoke pouring from the chimney. I pulled up beside a tree trunk with an ax stuck in the middle, cut the engine, and sat there listening to the motor cackle from its heat. I waited a couple of minutes, trying to decide just what the hell I'd say to Moreno when I saw him. There was no sign of any other cars, but I could see tire tracks leading around to the back of the property. I got out of the car and approached the cabin cautiously.

"Hello, anybody home?"

A man came out from around the back. He was big and had a bald bullet head, the sides crowned with a stubble of dark hair. He wore jeans and, despite the cold, just a plain white T-shirt. He was puffing like he'd just finished a workout, and the sinews were standing out like fishing lines along his biceps. He had a big black Doberman trailing at his heels.

"What do you want?" he asked bluntly.

I thought about reaching for the Beretta right away, but the dog looked like he'd jump at any sudden movement. I was sure this was the same man who directed me to drop the money off at the Bank of America Building. The same voice on Kostas' tape. "I'm supposed to meet Tim Riordan," I said, remembering the name of the realtor in the Cobb shopping center. "I think I took the wrong turn. Is this the Russo cabin?"

He ignored me, went over to the Granada and looked inside. Satisfied, he came back to me, his hands on his hips, breathing deeply. "Who are you?"

"Hamilton is the name. I'm looking for a summer cabin. Nice dog you've got there."

The Doberman was sniffing my pants leg.

"I think what you're looking for is over there."

I turned to see where he was pointing and suddenly the back of my head exploded.

Bogart, Dick Powell, William Powell, even Chester Morris. All the old-time private eyes. You know what they had that the modern generation doesn't? Hats. Good old heavy felt hats. They kept getting hit on the head, but bouncing right back up. My head felt like the Boston Celtics had been using it to run up the score on the Lakers.

Someone was slapping it back and forth, slowly, methodically, and painfully. I opened my eyes, then wished I hadn't. Old Baldy was leaning over me, smiling. His face was almost diamond-shaped, with a deeply cleft chin, bushy eyebrows, and thin lips under a slightly hooked nose.

"Well, the man of many names. What did you say it was? Hamilton? Then there was Walker, wasn't there?"

I guess he expected an answer, and when I didn't give him one, he took a small leather sap, the flat kind with all the weight at the end that cops aren't supposed to carry but always do in the back of their uniformed pants, and tapped the back of my head. I screamed and tried to stand up but only succeeded in raising my butt a few inches. I was tied down to an old wooden dining chair. The knots lashing my hands to the chair's arms looked professional.

"You did use the name Walker, didn't you?"

"Yes," I yelped as he brought the sap up again.

"That's better, Mr. Hamilton, Walker, and now Polo." He flapped my wallet in front of my face. "Is that your real name, friend?"

"Yeah, that's it and what—"

He brought the sap down with a snap, catching my little finger. I bit down on my lip to keep from screaming.

"Just answer the questions, Polo. Don't elaborate. What about this?" he asked, waving my inspector's badge.

"I used to be in the police department. I quit. I kept the badge."

He nodded and then stood back. "You ever see this clown?"

I turned my head and for the first time saw that we weren't alone. Richard Moreno and a young girl walked closer.

Moreno was wearing soiled bib overalls over a thermal knit undershirt. "I never saw the dude. Never."

The girl had hair the color of peeled carrots and skin so pale it looked like it had just been unbandaged. She had on dirty white pants and a bright blue sweatshirt.

"What about you, Mona?" Moreno asked. "You ever see him?"

"Uh-uh, not me."

Baldy bent over me again, tapping the sap on my smashed finger. "Well, I saw him. He's a good delivery boy. We could have a lot of fun with you, Polo. Take our time and get all the right answers. You look like a guy who likes to play games, but I don't have any time for games. So we're going to get this over with fast. I want to know how you found us, and I don't want to hear a lot of fucking bullshit, understand me?"

"I understand," I said, surprised at the squeakiness of my own voice.

"Pull down his pants," he said. Moreno and the girl undid my belt and pulled my pants and shorts down to my ankles. I kept an eye on Baldy. He went to the kitchen sink and came back with a can and a can opener.

"This is Satan's favorite. Alpo," he said as he opened the can and dumped the contents on my lap. "Chunky beef. Satan, come," he commanded, and I saw the dog hurtling across the floor, skidding to a stop in front of me, his open mouth inches away from my smeared crotch.

"Now, Polo. No games. You tell me how you got here and everything else you know about us, or Satan digs in."

I told him almost everything, starting with being bailed out of jail by Peckman. The only things I left out were Jill Ashbury and Yolanda identifying Cruz, and the tapes I'd taken from Kostas' apartment, with Baldy's voice, and his name, Bill, on it. He asked a few questions and I answered them honestly, my eyes never leaving the dog, whose eyes never left his hoped-for meal.

"What were you planning to do up here?"

"If I found Moreno, I was going to try and make a deal for the pictures. Peckman's willing to pay."

"How much?"

"We're open for offers."

He roughed the hair on the dog's skull while I held my breath, then snapped his fingers and pointed to the far corner of the room. The dog backed away immediately. "Wash him off," he told the girl, then he and Moreno left the room.

She used a cold towel from the sink and nothing had ever felt that good in my life. I tried to engage her in conversation, but she just shook her head and smiled at everything I said.

Baldy came back carrying a small leather bag. "You like our little Mona, eh, Polo? Well, you're going to get to know her much better."

He unzipped the bag and took out a syringe and a small bottle filled with a clear liquid. "Roll up his sleeve," he barked at the girl. He filled the syringe, pushed the plunger in just enough for a few drops to dribble out, then jabbed it roughly into my arm. He studied my eyes carefully. Whatever the drug was, it was fast-working. I could feel the effects almost immediately. The room was getting darker, fuzzier. I tried talking, but my tongue felt heavy.

Moreno was there again, using a knife to slash through the ropes tying me to the chair. I felt about as strong as a rag doll as they took off my shoes, pants, and shirt. Baldy said something I couldn't hear, and Moreno grabbed the girl by the hair and pulled her sweatshirt up, revealing a thin body with small, budding breasts. I felt my hands being guided to her breasts, saw somebody place them on the girl's body, then rake them down, leaving bright red scars and trails of blood. Suddenly the girl was down in front of me, on her knees, Moreno pushing her forward, and my hands were moved to her neck and squeezed. Two people were screaming. I thought one of them was me, but I couldn't be sure.

13

I think the pain woke me up. I was lying on my stomach,
my left hand twisted awkwardly under me. The little fin
ger that had been smashed by the sap was throbbing. I
slowly rolled onto one side and brought the finger up in
front of my face. It was all blue and red, and just trying to
wiggle it brought great shots of pain through the whole
arm area. I pulled myself up into a sitting position and
blinked rapidly, trying to clear my eyes. The first thing
that came into focus was Satan. He was sitting on his
haunches, head slightly lowered, mouth open, tongue
hanging out, and those awful damn teeth showing. I
started to feel like I was going under again, so I grabbed
the smashed finger and pressed. I moaned and cursed, but
at least I stayed awake. The room I was in was small,
unfurnished except for a mattress against the far wall.
There was someone on the mattress. I shivered and got to
my knees, realizing for the first time that I was naked.
God, it was cold. My breath hit the air like smoke signals.

The dog growled but didn't come after me. I rested on my knees for I don't know how long, alternating deep breaths with occasional pulls on the finger to bring me back to reality.

I finally struggled to my feet and, leaning against the wall all the way, made it over to the mattress. Mona lay on her back, arms akimbo, staring up at the ceiling. Her face was grainy white and puffy like boiled rice, her eyes looked like raisins thumbed deep into cookie dough. Her mouth was wide open, her tongue an obscene black protrusion falling to one side. I knelt down beside her, using my good hand to pull her eyelids down. The bruises on her neck stood out like blue black sapphires on the milky skin. She looked frozen. I thought if I flicked her flesh it would have pinged.

I got back to my feet and Satan growled, baring his full set of teeth. I backed away. He was positioned in front of a door. Apparently I could move around, but not anywhere near the door. No problem, Polo. Just a little dog between you and freedom. You and life, because if they killed the girl, it was a cinch they were going to leave me stretched out alongside her. I wondered how they were going to do it. Narcotics overdose? I killed Mona during a fit of passion, then OD'd? "Fuck," I said out loud. She was just another poor Debbie Bishop. Use her, then kill her. How many poor, stupid, dumb, helpless Debbie Bishops were there in the world? That's it, Polo, I told myself. Use the anger. You're a big, strong tough guy. You know all the angles. Now do something really clever. The only clever thing I could come up with was walking, slowly and painfully, trying to shake off the drugs.

I heard a car's motor. There was a small crack in the wall where the window was boarded up. I peeked through the slit and saw a beige van slowly negotiate its way over the dirt road and thankfully turn left toward Bottlerock Road. I could just make out the edge of the cabin where they'd questioned me. It looked to be a good two hundred yards away.

There was another door at the opposite end of the room. The rotting floorboards creaked under my weight as I half crawled toward it. Satan kept his eyes on me all the time but didn't interfere. If it turned out to be a closet, maybe I could hide in there and they wouldn't bother to look. Those are the stupid kinds of things you tell yourself at times like that. It wasn't a closet. It was a small bathroom: a toilet, and a battered metal stall shower. There was a bare patch on the pine wall where the basin used to be. I closed the door behind me. It had a lock of sorts, a single hook and eye that would take Satan about two jumps to knock down. I opened the door again. The dog was still at his position. He bent his head to one side and looked at me indifferently, as if no matter where I went or what I did, he'd be waiting. I closed the door again and used the useless lock. Like I said, those are the kinds of things you do at times like that. There were no windows in the bathroom. I tried the light switch and was surprised to see it worked. I tried the shower faucet. Another surprise. It worked. An ice-cold stream of rusty water coughed its way out of the pipes. I waited until it turned reasonably clear, then got in and gulped down as much as I could hold. The water had my teeth chattering in no time, but it also had me feeling more like I was alive. I took as much as I could, then turned the water off, shaking like a dog to try and get some of it off me.

I stood there shivering, trying to find some kind of a weapon. No mirrors, no pipes, not even a shower curtain that I might use to throw over the dog. Nothing. I sat on the toilet and prayed. It had been years, but the prayers came back quickly. As I prayed and shivered, my eyes darted back and forth looking for anything resembling a weapon; otherwise I'd just have to tackle Satan bare-handed. I remembered reading something when I was in the army. Something about attack dogs. Their weakest point was their legs. So the thing to do was have the dog jump for you, then you duck under him, grab his leg, give it the old el-twisto, and bingo, you win, he loses. In my condition a parakeet wouldn't have much trouble whip-ping me. I'd just about made up my mind to go out and give it a go, maybe use the mattress or poor Mona's body as a shield, when my brain finally started working and I saw the curtain rod. It was a thin tube of aluminum, or some such soft metal. It pulled away easily from the wall.

The rod was about three feet long, the ends rounded. I placed one end under the toilet seat and pressed down hard. The metal gave way and flattened out to a thin, jagged edge. My blood started pumping and I forgot about the cold. It was a weapon. Not much of one, but it'd have to do.

I rubbed my hands up and down the walls, trying to

dry them off as much as possible. One more quick prayer, then it was time to go to war.

I opened the door cautiously. Satan seemed to sense something was up, and he got to all fours and started padding toward me. I got down on my knees, down to his level, and braced my feet against the wall, the curtain rod lying next to me on the floor. I growled and waved my arms menacingly. Satan howled and came bouncing across the room. I picked up the rod as he made his leap and jabbed it at him with all the strength I had left, catching him in the chest. He seemed to hang there a moment, and I felt the rod being pushed back through my fingers by the force of his attack. Satan kept coming, pushing the rod back until the end hit the wall. Still the dog kept coming, impaling himself as he did so. He was wiggling madly back and forth, barking, his mouth foaming blood. I swung around and jumped on his back, riding him like a horse. I grabbed his thick neck and squeezed. His legs collapsed, and I kept squeezing, shoving him further toward the wall and into the curtain rod. Finally the great black body gave one last shudder and was still.

I stumbled across the room to the door Satan had guarded. It was locked but was so old and warped that it didn't take much effort to break it open. I pounded down the steps and started running toward my car, my feet oblivious to the rocky terrain.

Satan's barking must have alerted Moreno. He came loping down the road. I kept running toward the Granada. He was shouting something at me. I tried shutting everything out—Moreno, the pain, the cold. If the car's doors were locked, I was a dead man. *Get to the car, get to the car,* I kept telling myself. I slipped and skidded to the ground. Moreno was laughing at me. He went to the tree stump and freed the ax, and began swinging it back and forth slowly.

"You dumb asshole. Where the hell do you think you're going? Satan! Satan! What did you do to the dog, asshole?"

He came at me. I got to my feet and darted around the rear of the car, over to the driver's side. My hands slipped on the handle the first time, but I got the door opened and scrambled inside, reaching for the headrest.

Moreno grabbed my ankle and pulled. He was still laughing. I felt myself skidding on the vinyl seats. I kicked back and lunged for the headrest again, grabbing for the gun.

"You stupid shit, I told you, you ain't goin' nowhere, I'm gonna—"

The first shot caught him in the neck, the next in his chest. He tumbled backward, a look of astonishment on his face.

The car keys weren't in the ignition. I checked under the floor mat, the ashtray, then the sun visor. They weren't there.

For all I knew, old Bald Bill would be back any minute, and even with the gun I was in no shape to face him. I stepped over Moreno and searched his pockets. Nothing but a handkerchief and a pack of gum.

I hotfooted it over to the cabin. Smoke was still coming from the chimney. My shirt, pants, and shoes were layed out neatly on the kitchen table, along with my wallet, watch, badge, and the Beretta, all ready to be tossed next to my dead body so the cops wouldn't have any trouble identifying me. I dressed quickly. There was a rifle rack hanging on the wall over a large-console TV. There were two rifles that looked like .22's and a double-barreled shotgun. I put the .38 in my pocket and picked out the shotgun and a box of shells. As I loaded both barrels, I looked around the room. The kitchen contained nothing more than a dated stove, refrigerator, and sink. A ceiling fan, black with grease, turned in endless circles over the center of the room. The chair they had tied me in was set in front of the TV. The sound was off, but the set was on, the screen fluttering like a flag in the wind. A pot of coffee perfumed the air. I found a clean cup and used a dish towel to pick up the hot pot. The first sip scalded my tongue. A bottle of Ancient Age on the sink looked inviting as hell, but I didn't want to risk throwing alcohol on top of whatever it was they had pumped into me.

My breathing was almost back to normal now. I took the dish towel and went to the chair I'd been strapped into and wiped the arms down for prints. I was surprised there weren't indentations from my fingernails in the wood. I wiped the gun case and tried to recall anyplace else I'd touched.

Cradling the shotgun and carrying the coffee cup, I did a quick inventory of the place. There were two bedrooms. One was Spartan and clean, the single bed made up with precise hospital corners. No pictures on the wall; a nice-looking fruitwood armoire held nothing but a few sweaters and shirts. Nothing personal. The other room was a shambles. Clothing, both male and female, tossed everywhere. Cosmetics, cigarette butts, used Kleenex. Half-empty glasses with lipstick marks. A sandwich with a bite taken out.

The bathroom was barely big enough to turn around in, just a toilet, sink and shower.

There was no telephone, and I couldn't see anything that would give me any information on Bald Bill. It may have been there, but I didn't have time to look.

So what next? I asked myself reasonably, pouring another cup of coffee. What you've got here, Polo, is two dead bodies, both of which technically you killed. Three if you count the damn dog. So what do you do? Get to the cops, tell them everything, then spend the next few months going over and over it, while Peckman ignores you because the whole dirty story would have to come out, and the district attorneys of three counties fight over who has the right to be the lucky one that puts you on trial? I went outside and checked under the cabin. The usual array of tools, axes, saws, hammers. Some rope and four red gas cans. I sniffed. All the cans were full.

I brought a length of the rope over to Moreno, wrapped a few knots around his ankle, secured the other end to the Granada's bumper, and got in the car. It suddenly dawned on me that if the car didn't start, if they had done something clever with the engine, I'd be back up the famous creek again. The motor turned sluggishly, and I nursed it lovingly back to life, then drove back to the cabin with the girl's body. I thought of dragging Moreno inside, but what little adrenaline I had left in my system was fading fast. I rolled him under the stairs, then went back for the gas cans.

I felt bad about the girl but told myself I had no choice. I wiped the .38 clean, put it in her stiffening right hand, and pulled the trigger, the bullet plowing harmlessly into the mattress.

I splashed two of the gas cans inside, one underneath the stairs by Moreno, used my heel to scrape a trench some fifteen feet, poured the remaining gas into the trench, and dropped a match.

14

I was past Cobb Mountain by the time I saw the first fire truck steam past me. Yellow flashes of lightning flickered against the leaden sky, and rolling thunder cracked ominously over the hills. I stopped briefly in the little town of Calistoga, debating with myself over whether to drive the few miles to Martin's place in St. Helena or try and make it all the way back to the City. I was dying for another cup of coffee, something to eat, and a long hunk of sleep, but there was a possibility someone had spotted my car and a description of it would be put out to the police. The postal clerk would certainly remember me, but I had parked far enough away so that she shouldn't have seen the car. I found myself nodding off. I wound down the windows and inhaled fresh air. I couldn't afford to get stopped for some traffic violation in my condition.

It was after seven o'clock by the time I got to my

flat. I drove around the block a few times. There was no sign of cops of any kind. Or of a beige van.

Mrs. Damonte's venetian blinds flicked briefly as I passed her door. I knocked and she opened the door a bare crack. "Has anyone been looking for me?"

"Nopa."

Nopa. It was the closest thing to an English word I'd ever heard her use. I thanked her and walked up to my place. There were several calls waiting on the answering machine. Two from Peckman. Brief demands: "Call me right away." And again, "Call me right away, goddamn it!" A call from Roland Wilson saying that he had received some mail for José Cruz and wanted to know what to do with it, and a final one, "Lucky fucker." That was all, but I recognized the voice: old Bald Bill himself.

I stripped and took a quick, hot shower, then threw all the clothes I had worn—jacket, pants, socks, shoes, the works—in a paper bag, along with the shotgun shells, then dressed, packed a suitcase, and went to Pop's safe and dug out the rest of the money Peckman had given me, along with the .38 Magnum and my other "throw away" gun, a Spanish Llama 9mm automatic. I checked the gun's action. It seemed all right, though it hadn't been fired in years. One of the checkered grips was broken off, and the barrel blueing was down to bare metal in several places. Not pretty, but untraceable. I'd picked it up in some long-forgotten burglary investigation.

I called Jill Ashbury. "How would you like to nurse a sick man back to health?"

119

"It depends where his boo-boos are. What's the matter? You sound funny."

"I feel funny. I'd like to crash at your place. Afraid I won't be much fun though."

"What makes you think you were much fun last night? Come over, I'll be waiting."

I called Peckman. He was of his usual good cheer.

"Where the hell have you been?" he growled.

"You don't want to know. I tried getting hold of you last night and this morning."

Peckman's voice grew hoarse with anger. "You're working for me, not the other way around, Polo. Remember that." There was an uneasy pause, after which he said: "I think you did some good up in Sacramento. You scared the shit out of them. They want to deal. I've got them by the balls."

"Deal?"

"Talbot will drop out of the race. We'll back him for governor next year."

"That's the deal? Everyone is going to kiss and make up? What about the pictures? What about Debbie Bishop? What about—"

"Calm down, man. What are you yapping about? Who the hell is Debbie Bishop?"

I'd forgotten that Peckman didn't know about the dead girl. Either dead girl. I told him about Bishop's murder.

"You're sure it's the same girl that was in the pictures?"

"Positive. Now what do you think about your deal?"

120

"Hell, how do we know her death is connected to our problem? A little bitch like that, she could be in all kinds of shit, couldn't she? For all—"

"Listen, Peckman. You can bullshit yourself all you want, but don't try bullshitting me. Bishop isn't the only one."

"The only one what? What the hell are you talking about? You sound weird, Polo. Weird. Settle down or you'll be right back in Lompoc."

"I don't think so."

"Oh no?" There was a snap in his voice, like a whip cracking. "I can send you back there with a phone call. One call and your little dago ass is back in the slammer. Remember that!"

"No, you remember. Remember to go to your office tomorrow and look at that nice brass hole puncher on your desk. Turn it over and empty the waste tray. You'll find a lot of little white and yellow circles of paper. But you won't find any pictures of Barbara Martin's face."

"You prick," he shouted. "You no-good prick."

"Insurance, Peckman. Everyone needs insurance in this crazy world. I'll be in touch. Be careful of that deal with Talbot and Kostas. They're not alone. And the guy they've got working for them plays a brand of hardball you've never heard of."

I hung up before he could reply and went out to the car, stopping at a debris box on a construction site on California Street to dump the bag with the clothes and the shotgun.

Jill Ashbury greeted me cheerfully. "I've heard of

121

people aging rapidly, but this is ridiculous. What happened to you?"

I dropped my overnight bag and flopped on her couch. "You were too much for me last night, I guess."

She left and came back with a tall glass of champagne. "Want to tell me about it?" she asked.

"Nopa."

"What happened to your hand?"

I held my little finger up. It was swollen and blue, but the pain was only a dull throb now. "Someone thought it would look better like this, so he smashed it with a sap."

"You weren't kidding about the boo-boos, were you? Let's have an inventory."

She felt the back of my head, bringing a wince and an "Ouch."

"Finish the wine. I'll be right back."

I was dozing peacefully and opened my eyes just a crack when Jill started taking my shoes off, then the socks, then the pants. People taking my clothes off for me was becoming a habit. She got me to cooperate enough to get into a standing position, took off my coat and shirt, and guided me into the bathroom.

The floor was made of cedar slats; the walls were of gleaming white tile. An enormous Jacuzzi tub sat in the center, water churning, steam drifting up to the ceiling. The water was deliciously hot. There was a niche along the tub's wall so that you could sit with just your head sticking out of the water. I watched sleepily as Jill began undressing. She was wearing a black wrap-around dress;

underneath were a wisp of a black bra, a garter belt, and nylons.

"I thought garter belts were a thing of the past. Isn't this the panty hose generation?"

"The only thing panty hose are good for in my business is two-headed bank robbers," she said, pouring a jasmine-scented liquid into the tub. "Now sit back and close your eyes and relax. I won't let you drown."

15

Something smelled awfully good. I shook my head and blinked my eyes awake. Jill was putting a tray down on the bed. There was coffee, scrambled eggs, and croissants.

"What time is it," I mumbled, reaching for one of the rolls. It was steaming and dripping with butter.

"Almost eleven. You did a lot of yelling last night."

"I'll bet." I remembered some of my dreams. They had to do with Satan and his long white teeth. "I hope I didn't keep you up."

"You owe me one. Are you going to be all right?"

"No problem. And thanks. I appreciate everything."

"Here, maybe this will cheer you up a little."

She handed me a piece of heavy artist's paper. A pencil drawing of the face of an Oriental male with long dark hair and a pockmarked face stared back at me.

"That's José Cruz," Jill said. "I drew him from memory, with help from Yolanda."

"This is fantastic," I said truthfully. "Think you could try one more?"

She got her sketch pad and pencils, sat on the edge of the bed, and in less than thirty minutes had put together a lifelike portrait of the menacing head of Bald Bill.

"Fantastic," I repeated. "I had no idea you had such hidden talents."

"When you're a producer, you have to be able to do a little of everything. Which reminds me, I'm very late for work. Here's a key to the front door," she said, placing it on the food tray. "I'll be back around seven o'clock."

"I'm not sure just where I'll be, Jill. Not even sure if I'll be back tonight."

"Oh sure, the old wham-bam-thank-you-ma'am." One of her hands plucked at the mattress buttons through the sheets. "It's none of my business, Nick, but you look like you got in a little over your head. Keep the key and take care of yourself."

She was gone and I was finished with breakfast before I noticed that my little finger was bound up in a professional-looking splint. I got out of bed and went over to a full-length mirror and took stock of myself. Jill had used some foul-looking orange ointment on the cuts and scratches. The back of my head was still sore, but all in all I looked reasonably presentable. I padded barefoot into the kitchen, poured some more coffee, and skimmed through the morning paper. There was nothing about the fire or murders at Cobb and no new stories on Barbara Martin.

My first inclination was just to get out of town—fly over to Hawaii for a week and bake on the beaches, wait until things blew over—but trouble like this would have no difficulty in blowing across a little thing like the Pacific Ocean. Besides, if Bald Bill and I were going to be at war, I wanted him on my own turf.

Jill's bathroom was better equipped than most beauty salons. I found a fingernail clipper and a file and cut my nails down as far as they would go, then used a scrub brush on them till they were almost raw. I wondered how many scrubbings it would take to get rid of the last microscopic remains of poor Mona and that miserable dog.

The first move on the agenda was to switch cars. I turned in the Granada and rented a new T-bird, silver in color, just like Kostas'. I wasn't concerned about parking tickets now, just staying alive, and a little more speed might help. Besides, Bald Bill knew the Granada.

The rain had let up and the sky was bright blue and filled with popcorn clouds as I pointed the T-bird toward Berkeley.

Roland Wilson was still plugging away at his piano.

"I had a lesson scheduled for today. He never showed up. Never even bothered to call. The young are like that nowadays, aren't they, Mr. Polo?"

"Thanks for calling me, sir. Did something come in for Mr. Cruz?"

"Yes. From a photography studio. I thought they might help you and Miss . . . what was her name?"

"Jill Ashbury."

"Yes." His eyebrows knitted together. "Charming

126

lady. You know, I'm positive I've seen her somewhere before, but for the life of me I just can't remember where."

"Where's Mr. Cruz's mail?"

He shuffled over to a rolltop desk, the top littered with figurines of cats and stacks of mail. "Here it is. I hope this helps you."

It was a typical business mailer, with the clear plastic cutout on the envelope showing Cruz's name. It was from an outfit called Bastiani Prints on University Avenue. I tore the envelope open before Wilson could protest. It was a bill in the amount of $36.80 for photo development.

Bastiani Prints was a small storefront with a faded poster of a pretty girl in a bikini bouncing a beach ball and smiling her teeth out for Kodak Film in the window. A big burly man with a mop of curly hair was behind the counter. I handed him Cruz's bill and reached for my wallet.

"José wanted me to pick these up for him."

He eyed me suspiciously, then looked at the two twenties on the counter and shrugged. "How is he?" he asked while picking through an alphabetized filer.

"Okay. He'll be out of town for a couple of weeks. Film job down in L.A."

He handed me two thick envelopes and made change from the twenties. "You know him well?"

"No. Just a business acquaintance. Why?"

He screwed up one side of his face as if he were

squinting through a telescope. "Well, he was just a little strange, that's all. Some of his pictures he had to handle himself. He knew what he was doing, all right, no doubt about that, and he paid me good money to use the developing tanks, so I shouldn't gripe. Don't know what he was worried about. You should see some of the stuff we run through here. Twenty years ago we'd have been busted by the vice squad, but not now. Anything goes, I guess, huh?"

"Just about anything," I agreed. "Was Cruz alone when he came in to do his developing?"

"Yeah. I don't like anybody handling my machines, but like I said, he was a pro, otherwise there's no way I'd let him back there," he said, pointing a finger behind his back to the rear of the shop that was closed off by a curtained wall.

I thanked him, picked up my change, and went back to the car. The first set of prints was pretty routine; shots of various locations in San Francisco that had been photographed thousands of times before: Coit Tower, the bridges, old Fort Point, the section of Lombard Street that has been heralded as the crookedest street in the world, the cable cars. All the pictures were clear, bright, well framed, and would look good on the fronts of postcards.

The second set of prints was something else. Debbie Bishop and Richard Moreno on the beach, he with his shirt off, she in shorts and a halter, running, laughing, smiling stupidly as they ate hot dogs. I couldn't tell just which beach it was. There were some more pictures of them in a wooded area, a series of shots in which they were kissing, taking off each other's clothes. Again there was no way to tell just where the pictures were taken. I wondered if the location was Cobb Mountain, or Golden Gate Park where they found Debbie's body.

I drove back to San Francisco and was mid-span on the bridge when a Count Basie record was interrupted by a news flash: the mayor of San Francisco had committed suicide.

16

A memorial service was held in the rotunda in City Hall. The casket, a massive oak and brass affair, was centered exactly under the center of the magnificently carved dome. Uniformed policemen and firemen stood at uncomfortable attention alongside as the mourners filed by. Hundreds of floral pieces hung from the stone walls, their sweet scents mixing with the smell of the crowd: sweat, damp raincoats, and fear.

The casket was closed. Barbara Martin had ended her life dramatically by placing the barrel of her ex-husband's shotgun in her mouth and pulling the trigger. According to the newspaper accounts, there was no doubt it was suicide. Only her prints had been found on the weapon and she'd left a brief note in her own handwriting: "I'm sorry. God forgive me."

Walter Peckman stood at the end of the casket, shaking hands with people as they passed by. His face had a cracked-cement look. I joined the mourners, a mixed group of neatly dressed older people, youngsters in jeans, workmen in Big Ben's and hickory shirts, nuns, priests, rabbis, ministers.

Peckman was working the line like the professional politician he was: a handshake, a pat on the back, a murmured "Thank you for coming" or "Yes, please pray for her."

"I've been trying to get ahold of you for two days," I whispered as he grabbed my hand.

"Later."

"Where? I want to see you today."

He looked nervously down the line of mourners. He coughed, phlegm rattling in his throat. "After the funeral. At the B.V."

I moved along, finding an open spot near the marble staircase, and surveyed the crowd. Twenty minutes later Lawrence Talbot made an appearance. The people standing in line parted for him as if he were Moses at the Red Sea. He went right to the coffin, made the sign of the cross, and then stood next to Peckman, tall, erect, a sorrowful look on his handsome features as he consoled a sobbing elderly woman.

On an average day the Buena Vista pours thirty-six quarts of Irish whiskey. On St. Patrick's Day they probably double that figure. That afternoon the place was almost empty. Barbara Martin's death had left the whole city in a state of mourning. The legend goes that Irish coffee was invented one cold, foggy morning behind the plank at the Buena Vista. It was one of those rare places a tourist must see, one that served good food and honest drinks and got a steady share of local customers.

I sipped through the heavy whipped cream and took a long swallow of the hot coffee and whiskey. It was a day to mark everyone's mood: dark, threatening, and cold. I was on my second Irish when Peckman showed up. He was dressed for the weather, a heavy black overcoat, black homburg, and was carrying a tightly rolled umbrella.

"What a fucking day," he said, leaning on the bar next to me. "Give me one of those too, buddy."

We waited in silence for his drink. He swallowed it almost in a gulp, wiping some cream from his lips with the back of his hand. "Let's take a walk."

We crossed the little park where the cable cars turn around to climb their way back up halfway to the stars and walked to the Aquatic Pier, a long hook of concrete that extended out into the bay. On a nice day the pier was loaded with fishermen and sightseers. Today we had it to ourselves.

"What do you want, Polo?"

"What do you think I want? I saw Talbot at City Hall. Where was Kostas?"

"Kostas is out," he said, stopping to lean over the railing and look down into the pewter-colored water.

"Out of what? Out of the country? Out of his mind?"

"Larry dumped him. This was before Barbara killed herself. He had no idea what was going on. It was that fucking Kostas. He hired some guy to get some dirt on Barbara. I guess he dug around and couldn't find anything, so he set her up. But even Kostas didn't know how far this crazy would go. He didn't know anything about the pictures until you showed up and showed them to Talbot."

"Who was this guy Kostas hired?"

Peckman shrugged his shoulders. "I don't know. Just some jerk he knew in the service."

"Where's Kostas now?"

"I don't know, damn it. What difference does it make now? Barbara's dead. It's over." He turned around and pushed the tip of his umbrella into my chest. "Don't worry, you can keep all the money I gave you, and you're square with Lompoc. You're out. Served all your time, no strings."

I pushed the umbrella away and grabbed him by the throat. His homburg sailed away into the bay. "That's it!" I shouted angrily as I pushed him back to the pier wall. "You mean you expect it to just lie there? What about the people who have been killed? What about the pictures? Do you think this bastard is going to let it just drop, just because the poor woman killed herself? You think you can just say it's over, and it's over?"

"Easy, easy," he said nervously. "Listen, I loved that lady. She was something special. She was class with a capital *C*. There was going to be no way to stop her, the Senate, maybe vice president, maybe the top job. She would never make the dumb mistakes the others did. But she's dead. What the hell am I supposed to do? She killed herself! What am I supposed to do about that?"

"What made her do it?"

Peckman drank in deep drafts of the icy air. "She called me. There were more pictures. Delivered right to her house. They wanted more money. Fifty thousand this

133

time. There was a note saying that this would be it. Fifty thousand and all the negatives would be destroyed. I jumped Talbot. He swore he had nothing to do with it, volunteered to take a lie-detector test. I'm telling you, Larry was as pissed as I was, Polo."

"Did you see the pictures?"

"No. Barbara burned them. She was upset, sure, but I never thought she'd kill herself. Shit. What a waste."

"I want to talk to Kostas."

"What for. The guy's a loser. Larry dumped him. Hasn't seen him for days. What good is it going to do now? Barbara's dead. Let her rest in peace, for God's sake."

I slammed Peckman against the concrete bulkhead. "For God's sake, or for yours? You and Talbot, good old Larry, you're really buddy-buddy now, aren't you?"

"Don't push it, Polo. I can still cause you a lot of—"

I hit him hard, right in the middle of his big belly. He doubled over in pain, and I pushed him over the bulkhead, grabbing him by the seat of the pants so that his feet were dangling off the ground and his head was pointed down, looking right into the bay.

"Listen, you miserable piece of shit. You call your good friend Larry Talbot. Tell him I'm coming up to see him. I want Kostas. Understand me?"

"You've got to be crazy, you can't—"

I hoisted him up a few more inches, so that he was tottering, half on and half off the wall. Just a gentle push now and he would be on his way to the murky gray water. "You set me up as a patsy in this deal from day one, Peckman. I was expendable, wasn't I? Well, no more." I reached between his legs, grabbed his crotch and squeezed. He screamed out, his arms flaying wildly, trying to keep his balance.

"I've got you by the balls in more ways than one, Walter old boy. So don't fuck with me anymore. If you and Talbot want to jump into bed and make beautiful politics together, then you better keep me happy."

I let go of him and he scrambled back off the wall's edge, dropping to his knees, shivering.

"What about the money?" I asked.

"What money?"

"The fifty thousand. Where was it supposed to be delivered?"

"Shit, I don't know, I haven't even thought about it."

"Well, think about it. Even with Barbara Martin dead, those pictures and the tapes are worth money to this bastard."

Peckman struggled to his feet, confidence returning to his voice. We were talking money now, something he understood. "Who the hell would buy the pictures now?"

"You. Who is the executor of Martin's estate?"

His eyes brightened. "I am. It's all cut and dried. No kids, no spouse. Most of the money goes to charities, the rest to a half-sister who lives in New York, and some nephews and nieces."

It started to rain again. I bent over and picked up his umbrella and opened it. "He'll be contacting you then. For the fifty thousand. Tell him you'll deal, but stall him, tell him it will take a little time to come up with the cash."

135

"What makes you so sure he'll call me?"

"Because you're the man with the purse strings now. He's gone to an awful lot of trouble. Killed a couple of people, taken some big risks, and now his golden goose is gone. So he'll come to you, thinking that you were Barbara's friend, and that you'll pay just to keep her reputation intact. You're his last big chance. Either you, or he peddles the stuff to the porno underground. There wouldn't be much money in that, but that wouldn't stop him."

"Yeah, well tell me something. What's in it for you, Polo? Huh? What's in it for you? You met Barbara once that I know of. Why the big hero act? There's got to be some goodies in this for you. How the hell do I know you're not working with this guy now, setting me up, helping him put the squeeze on me."

I swear that if the water hadn't been so rough, if the tide wasn't running so swiftly, if I thought there was even a ten percent chance that Peckman could swim to shore, I'd have dumped him into the bay right then. He must have seen something in my face, because he backed away, holding up his hands.

"Okay, okay. Don't get mad. I just had to ask. Don't get hot."

"You call Talbot. Right away. I want to see him at his office tomorrow morning. Then you call me when you get contacted about delivering the money."

He started to protest, then mumbled an "okay" and stalked off in the rain. I was glad he left the umbrella.

17

"Mr. Polo will be working in Mr. Kostas' office, Linda. Extend him every courtesy. Please answer any of his questions as if they were coming from me. Any documents he requires, provide them."

"Yes, Senator Talbot."

Linda got up from behind her desk. "This way, sir."

She was wearing a buttery yellow angora sweater and a camel-colored skirt today. I followed her across the room.

"Let me know if there's anything else you need," Talbot said, retreating back to his office.

Linda opened a door and extended an arm. "Here it is."

Kostas' office was about the same size as Talbot's, but where the senator's was clean, tidy, almost monkish, Kostas' was jammed with mismatching colored filing cabinets, floor-to-ceiling bookshelves, a copy machine, and a half dozen chairs strewn around a massive oak desk, the top of which was littered with three telephones, an IBM typewriter, a beer stein stuffed with pens and pencils, and file folders with papers and newsclippings spilling out.

Linda closed the door behind her with a soft bang. "May I ask you a question?"

"Fire away."

"Just who the devil are you? First you're a Mr. Walker, you come here out of the blue one morning and everyone goes into a panic. Now you come walking back as a Mr. Polo and are given carte blanche. So who are you? What agency are you with? FBI? CIA? Or some alphabet I've never heard of?"

I flopped down in the padded chair behind Kostas' desk. "None of the above, Miss. . . ?"

"Bradbury." She folded her arms across her chest and glared down at me.

"I'm just a private investigator." I gave her one of my cards and, when that didn't impress her, took out my wallet and showed her my license.

"Why all the charades?" she asked.

"Were you friendly with Kostas?"

Some color came to her cheeks. "What do you mean by friendly?"

"Just that. He's missing. I'd like to find him. Tell me, what kind of guy is he to work for?"

"I don't actually work for Jim. I work for Senator Talbot. But I did do some things for him—typing, filing. He liked to do a lot of his own correspondence. Sometimes he'd bring in someone from the typing pool."

"Yeah, but what kind of guy is he?"

She settled primly into a wooden side chair. "Hard-working, likes to think he's macho, I guess, but he can be nice. He has a good sense of humor."

I tried measuring Linda for one of the dresses in Kostas' closet. "Have you ever been to his apartment?"

The color bounced back into her cheeks. "I'm married, Mr. Polo. Fourteen years to the same man. Really married, and I don't think I—"

I held up a hand in mock surrender. "Okay, okay. I was just asking. You're an attractive woman, he's a good-looking guy. It was just a question." I leaned forward. "Look, Linda. Let's have a truce, huh? I'm trying to find the guy. For your boss. There's nothing personal in my questions. When did you last see Jim Kostas?"

"Ummmm, four days ago, I guess it was."

"The day Mayor Martin killed herself?"

"I . . . I guess it was. Why, is there some connection?"

"Not that I'm aware of. How did he seem that day?"

"Well, upset of course. I think he knew Mrs. Martin slightly, not as well as . . ."

"As Talbot. I know. What time of the day was it when you saw him last?"

"After lunch. He heard about Mrs. Martin on the radio. Came in to tell me about it."

"And Talbot wasn't here?"

"No, he was at the capitol."

"How did Kostas react to Martin's death?"

She wiggled back into her chair and stared at the ceiling. "He seemed shocked. Really shocked. Told me to get ahold of Senator Talbot right away."

"And you haven't seen him since then?"

"No, though he must have come back to the office that night. A lot of things were missing from his office."

"Oh? Like what?"

"Some files, his business calendar, checkbooks, and that picture." She pointed a long finger to a bare spot on the wall. "There was a photograph of Jim and some of his army buddies from Vietnam there."

"What did Kostas do in the army?"

She seemed surprised by my question. "Why, he was in intelligence, with Senator Talbot. Of course, the senator was a colonel then. They were both in Army Intelligence."

"Wrong. I was in Vietnam too, and believe me, there wasn't anyone in the whole damn army with any intelligence."

She smiled. "Would you like a cup of coffee?"

"Love one. And Linda, if Kostas wanted to hire someone to do a job for him, or for the senator, sort of a security, or intelligence job, you know, get the rundown on someone, who would he use?"

"Security? Gee, I don't know."

"How would he pay for it? Say this was something he wanted to do without Talbot knowing about it, something he thought could be better done without bothering you or Talbot."

"Like I said, he liked to handle a lot of things himself. He had his own office checking account. That's one of the things that is missing—the checkbook, register, all the old canceled checks."

"Have you any idea where Kostas might go? Who his friends are, that kind of thing?"

She shrugged her shoulders. "He made a fairly heavy pass at me when I first came to work here. I let him know how I felt about it. Since that time we were rather cordial to each other."

I showed her the composite drawings of Bald Bill and José Cruz. "Ever see either of these men?"

She took her time looking them over.

"No, I don't think so."

The composites had drawn a blank from Talbot too. So what was the connection between Kostas and Bald Bill? I had a feeling the answer was right there in his office. Or had been before he came back and stripped the files and took the checkbooks. I stared at the faded blank spot on the wall. Kostas didn't seem to be the sentimental type, so why take the picture? Because Bill was in it with him? Or Cruz? Or both?

I rummaged through his desk and cabinets, coming up with nothing but a set of keys. I was hoping they were for his apartment; I didn't feel like pushing my luck as a burglar again.

Linda poked her head in and told me I had a phone call. "Line number 2381," she said, pointing to one of the phones on Kostas' desk, a multiline job with one yellow button flashing.

Peckman was the only one who knew I was visiting Kostas' office, so I picked up the receiver confidently and asked, "Any news, Walter?"

"Hello, Lucky," came the now familiar voice. "Still sticking your nose into places it doesn't belong, I see. I guess you'll never learn."

"You know how it is, Bill. We Vietnam vets just have a tough time adjusting, don't we?"

There was a long, chilly pause, then he said, "You're pushing your luck pretty far, friend."

"What did you want to talk about, Billy?"

Talbot came into the room. His face was ashen and he walked with his arms straight down, like a prisoner.

"I just spoke to Talbot and your old buddy Walter Peckman, Polo. They're going to get a package together for me. Since you did such a good job as a delivery boy last time, I want you to handle this one too."

"Get a new puppy yet?"

"You're pretty cocky for someone the police are after for killing two people."

"I had help on one. The other was easy."

"We'll have to have a chat about that sometime. I want to know—"

"Listen," I cut in, "I'm pretty busy now, Bill. Call me back in a few minutes, will you? And by the way, say hello to José Cruz for me."

I cut the connection before he could reply. Talbot was leaning shakily against the wall.

"You talked to him?" I said.

"Yes. He says he's sent some photographs to my home. Says he addressed them to my wife. He knew her name, Catherine, even her nickname, Kitty. He knows my daughter's name, for God's sake!"

"Are the pictures of Barbara Martin?"

"Yes." He closed his eyes and shook his head. "I don't know why. My wife met Barbara a few times, but she really didn't know her. Why bother my wife?"

"Just to show you he has power. Have you called your wife?"

"No."

"Call her. Tell her you're expecting some threatening mail. Tell her not to open anything until you get there, or can send someone down to pick the stuff up. Tell her not to touch any of the mail—fingerprints, that kind of thing."

"Good idea, good idea," he said, heading for the door.

"Wait a minute, Talbot. The man on the phone. What did he want from you?"

"What else? Money. Fifty thousand dollars. Can you imagine that? Where am I going to get fifty thousand in cash."

"Or what?"

He looked at me with a dazed expression on his face.

"Or what will he do if you don't come up with the money?" I explained.

"He says he'll leak the pictures, along with a story that I set Barbara up. That I was responsible for her suicide."

"Did he say anything about Kostas?"

"Kostas? No, I don't think so."

"That picture that was on the wall. The one with Kostas and some buddies in Vietnam. Did you know any of the other people in the picture?"

"No, I don't think they were even in our unit. Jim was sort of a liaison man between us and the front lines. I was stuck in the office most of the time."

Stuck in the office. Can you believe that one? I wondered what he did when the air conditioner didn't work, or the roof leaked, or they ran out of ice at the officer's club. Things like that we never had to worry about out in the jungle.

"The man that called. Did he know I was here, or did you tell him?"

"I told him," he said defensively. "I thought you'd want to talk to him."

"Thanks. Go on. You better call your wife."

He mumbled something, turned, and hurriedly left the room.

I hadn't thought of Vietnam for a while. It was something that you tried to push as far back into your mind as possible. But it came back in a flood now: the fear, the stench, the corruption, the confusion, and the waste. The total waste of lives and flesh. And guys like Talbot making decisions while they were stuck in their offices.

I swiveled the chair around and stared at the blank spot on the wall, remembering different faces, different places. I remembered guys from Special Services coming into our zones, usually alone, except for their dog. The dogs were mostly German shepherds. But there were a couple of Dobermans. They used them on the trails, sniffing out Charlie's booby traps, his tunnels. The dogs were friendly mutts once you got to know them, but not their masters. They were something else: tough, mean, loners who seemed to like what they were doing. Guys like Bald Bill.

I called Peckman's number. He answered on the first ring.

"Jesus, I just talked to that nut. What the hell did you say to him."

"He wasn't happy?"

"That's putting it mildly, Polo. He's pissed at you, but he wants money from me. Fifty thousand dollars."

"You're in good company. He wants the same from Talbot. What did he threaten you with?"

"Same shit as before. Says he'll release the pictures. Claims we haven't seen the real good ones yet, whatever the hell that means. Says he can prove that I set her up. Me and Talbot together."

"Did you?"

"Fuck you, Polo," he screamed. "I told you how I felt about Barbara. She was family to me."

"Take it easy. Save your anger for him. Talbot didn't take it very well. Why don't you call him, try and calm him down. I don't want him cracking up on us. What's the timetable for the delivery of the money?"

"He wants it like yesterday. I explained to him that it would take some time, that I can't just pull it out of a desk drawer."

"Keep stalling him. Tell him you'll cooperate, but that you've got problems—probate, the income tax people, that kind of thing."

"I won't be lying. Cash. Shit, who has cash anymore?"

"You can find it, Walter. You're a man of great influence. You got me out of prison, didn't you?"

"Don't remind me." There was a long pause. "What are you planning? What's going on in that twisted dago mind of yours? You getting a cut out of this?"

145

"I'm just trying to keep you alive, Peckman. I told you before. This guy plays for keeps. You cross him and he'll kill you. And enjoy doing it."

"You really think so?" he asked, an edge of panic starting to filter into his voice.

"I'm positive. Give Talbot a call. I'll keep in touch."

I found a piece of paper with Talbot's impressive letterhead on top, used Kostas' typewriter and pecked out a short note to Kostas' landlord, and brought it over to Talbot to sign. He was on the phone, one hand rumpling his hair, the other nervously sliding up and down the receiver. I pushed the paper under his nose and he looked up blankly.

"Sign it," I said, handing him a pen. He tucked the phone under his chin, scanned the paper, then scribbled his name and handed it back to me.

18

Kostas' landlord was a short, pinch-faced man in his sixties. He read the letter and scratched his head, rearranging the thin gray strands that had been carefully sprayed in place.

"Gee, I don't know about this," he said.

I showed him my shiny police badge. "I could go through the trouble of getting a warrant, but I thought this would be easier."

"Oh, you're a cop. Why didn't you say so in the first place."

I followed him to Kostas' apartment. The damage I'd done to his front door was still visible; the wood had been replaced but wasn't painted yet.

"See this," the manager said. "Some damn punks broke in here a few days ago." He twisted his head to look at me as he unlocked the door. "Is that what this is all about?"

"I wish I could tell you, pal, but you know how it is."

He opened the door and I stepped inside and sniffed, expecting the worst, but there was nothing unusual, just the same stale, musty smell as last time. I asked the manager to stay where he was while I briefly checked the bedrooms and bathroom. No sign of Kostas, but then I didn't really expect there would be. Not alive, anyway.

I shook the manager's hand, thanked him for his help, and closed the door on him before he could protest. I put Kostas' coffee machine to work, then went to work myself, slowly and methodically this time.

In two hours the only things of interest I'd come up with were a .25 caliber pistol, with plastic pearl grips, the kind of weapon they used to call "a ladies gun" in the old movies—it was smaller than my Beretta—and a sandwich bag of white powder that looked and tasted like cocaine. They were both hidden in a pair of cowboy boots in Kostas' closet. Other than that, zip. No personal papers, no checkbooks, airline tickets, or that photo album I'd seen last time with the pictures of Kostas in Vietnam. The big automatic that I'd dropped in the toilet was long gone too. I dumped the cocaine in the toilet, gave it a flush, and pocketed the little automatic.

I added some of Kostas' bourbon to the last of the coffee and tried to figure out my next move. Wait for Bill to call the turn, set up a meeting for the money, and try and take him out? Take him out. I was starting to sound like a hit man. But that's what it had boiled down to, your good old basic him or me. Bill would take the money and forget about Peckman and Talbot. But not me. No, I had seen him, and so far everyone who knew what he looked like was dead. I wouldn't take any kind of odds on Kostas still being alive. Maybe Cruz was, or had I marked the Filipino for an early grave when I told Bill to say hello for me? Bill hadn't liked that, me knowing Cruz, or knowing his first name. Was he worried? Sweating a little? I hoped so.

I used Kostas' phone, dialed information, and got the number for the Lake County Sheriff's Office.

A flat, bored voice answered the phone.

"Lake County sheriff."

"Hi, Inspector Jack Harris, San Francisco Police Department. Is anyone who's handling that mess at old Rothman's around?"

"Yes, Inspector. Detective Hollings is in charge. I'll transfer you."

Hollings was cordial at first, checking me out by asking if I knew a few S.F. cops, two of which I did, because they existed, the third of which I didn't, because he didn't. Hollings finally seemed satisfied that I was who I said I was.

"How can I help you, Jack?" he asked.

"I've got a missing kid." I described Mona as best I could. "Her name's Jane Kingsberry. Someone told me she had moved up to the Lake County area with some bum. I thought there might be a connection."

"We haven't identified the girl's body yet. Got the dead man's name if that'll help." I could hear him rummaging through some papers. "Richard Moreno. He's got

149

a record in Frisco." He gave me Moreno's criminal identification number.

"What do you think happened? Double homicide?"

"Hard to tell. He was shot, no doubt about that. The girl, or what was left of her, was holding a gun. Gun's all fucked up from the fire. Just bones left on her, not much more on Moreno. Coroner's having a hell of a time coming up with much. We think they had some kind of a fight, she shot him, may have tried to burn him up, got caught by the fire herself. Shit, it's one of those tricky ones. You know how they are."

"I sure do. No other suspects?"

"Yeah, some crazy deal about a process server up here looking for Moreno the day he was killed, but I haven't been able to get anything on him so far."

"Well, if I get any more information on my missing girl, I'll get in touch." I thanked him and hung up before he could ask for my number.

So maybe Bill was right. I was lucky. At least as far as Mona and Moreno went.

19

Talbot and Peckman were on pins and needles. Bald Bill had given them two days to get the money up, or another "or else." He told Peckman to look under the hood of his Cadillac. Peckman did and found a strange substance stuck to the car's starter. It turned out to be nothing but silly putty, but it had made a believer out of Peckman. On Talbot he used another photograph. This one of Talbot's wife sunbathing in the back of their home by the swimming pool. Talbot claimed it had to have been taken with a telephoto lens, so maybe José Cruz was still alive and well. Anyway, the money suddenly became available.

I was getting used to seeing luggage stuffed with large sums of money; still, no matter how many times you see it, it's an impressive sight.

Peckman handed me the bag as if it contained three-week-old baby diapers. "Give it to him and let's get the damn thing over with," he said, then walked directly to the bar and fixed himself a stiff drink.

We were in Peckman's office again, back where it had all started for me.

Lawrence Talbot was sitting across the room staring at the suitcase, a thin film of sweat spreading over his forehead. "Ah, don't you think we should get a receipt or something, Walter?"

"Fuck you, Talbot," I said, opening the case and counting the money. It was all neatly stacked, one hundred packets of fifties and hundreds, each adding up to a thousand dollars.

Peckman finished his drink. It didn't look like his first of the day, and it was early. "You will be careful with that, won't you, Nick?"

"I'll treat it like it was my own," I told him truthfully, because either I was going to end up with the money or I was going to end up dead.

Peckman poured himself a short one, finished it in a gulp, turned to Talbot and said, "It's time for us to get out of here." He offered me his hand. "Good luck. Let us know how it went as soon as you can."

"You'll be the first. Remember, no calls. Not to anyone until you hear from me."

He nodded, took one last look at his office, and went to the door. A uniformed policeman was outside waiting for him.

"Come on, Talbot," he said irritably. "Let's get going."

Talbot gave me a mournful look, then moved to the door, like a man leaving a funeral.

I looked at my watch. Ten minutes to eleven, right on schedule. There was a limousine waiting on the ramp by a little-used exit on Grove Street. Both Peckman and Talbot were dressed in overcoats and hats. They'd be in sight for no more than a couple of seconds, then on their way to the airport and a private jet, whose flight plans were filed for Los Angeles but whose destination was Seattle, Washington. Talbot's wife and daughter were waiting for him at the plane. Peckman, a bachelor like myself, only had himself to worry about.

Bald Bill was due to call at eleven. I wet the end of a rubber suction cup attached to a three-foot cord, stuck it onto the phone's receiver, then plugged the other end of the cord into a small microcassette recorder. Cheap, but effective.

I settled into Peckman's chair and waited. The only sound in the office was the creaking of the chair as I slowly rocked back and forth.

The call came in at four minutes after the hour.

"Hi, Bill," I said cheerfully, punching the recording button.

"Hello, Lucky. Let me talk to Peckman."

"No can do. He's gone."

"Gone?"

"Long gone, Bill. So let's cut the shit and get this over with, okay?"

"You really like to push that luck of yours, don't you?"

I didn't answer, and finally he said, "All right, here's what you do. At twelve o'clock be at the phone booth at Jefferson and Taylor, across from the Fisherman's Grotto."

"Sorry, Bill. I can't make it by twelve. In fact, I'm tied up for the rest of the day. It'll have to be tomorrow."

His voice dripped icicles. "Who do you think you're fucking with? You try and play games with me and you are a dead man. Dead, do you hear me?" He shouted so loud that I had to hold the phone away from my ear.

"Billy, calm down. Relax. This is a business deal now. You'll get the money, or most of it, anyway."

"Most of it? Listen you dumb prick, and listen real good. If that money isn't delivered today—"

"Bill, I've got expenses too, you know. And you've given me a pretty hard time, you can't deny that, so I figure I've earned about twenty-five thousand dollars of the money."

"You son of a bitch. You are a dead man. Right now."

"Be reasonable. I'll settle for ten thousand, how's that?"

"The money, today, Polo. All of it."

"You're getting repetitious. Now listen good. I've got a few more things to do to get all the money together. Call me at my place tomorrow. Leave a message on my machine. And don't try stopping by early, Bill, because I won't be there. Then we'll meet and discuss the money."

He started swearing and I cut him off.

"Don't get any dumb ideas. You'll get your money, you just give me the pictures and the videotapes, all of them, including the negatives, and I'll give you the money. Hell, if you're going to be such an asshole about it, I'll just hit Peckman and Talbot up for twenty-five

154

thousand, tell them you wanted more, or I'll just sell them the pictures I have."

"What pictures? What are you talking about?"

"The first batch you sent. Peckman showed them to me. I made copies. What the hell, it's all a game isn't it? I need money and protection too. And speaking of protection, I've got a little more than you think. I've got a composite drawing of you that's as good as a Polaroid. I know you were in 'Nam with Kostas and Cruz. I've got a set of pictures that Cruz took of Moreno and Debbie Bishop. I've got a lovely composite of Cruz too, along with a recording I'm making of this conversation. All of it will be in a nice package ready for the cops, along with a report saying that your prints are probably all over that cabin in Lake County. I guess that was your room with the nicely made up bed and the neat drawers, huh, Bill? Moreno and the girl were kind of sloppy, weren't they?"

There was a cold silence of twenty seconds. When he spoke again, his voice was controlled, but there was no disguising the anger.

"You sure do like to play dangerous games. I'll call you tomorrow at ten. If I don't get the money tomorrow, I'll release the pictures. All of them. All over this fucking town. Then I'll find you and kill you, Polo. Real slow. It might be worth losing the money to get you. You were right about 'Nam. I learned a lot of things over there. Killing was one of them. So you get me that money tomorrow."

He broke the connection, and when I put the receiver down, I realized it was damp with sweat.

I picked up the case with the money and started to leave, then stopped, went back to Peckman's desk, and opened his humidor. It was empty. He trusts me with a hundred thousand dollars but not his cigars.

It was Saturday, so City Hall was empty. A guard unlocked the front door for me, and I walked down to my car, a new Chevrolet I'd just picked up from Hertz an hour ago. Two motorcycle cops were parked next to the car. They eyed me suspiciously.

"Are you Nick Polo?" one of them asked.

"Right," I said, unlocking the Chevy. "Just escort me across Market Street. I'll take it from there."

They both shrugged their shoulders in unison like robots and kicked the bike motors on. The weather had changed for the better and Civic Center Plaza was crowded. Several Chinese kids were trying to launch a long, colorful kite in the shape of a dragon, and a group of teenagers with their shirts off were tossing a Frisbee back and forth. I wondered where Bill was. He should be somewhere close. Watching. And mad as hell.

I followed the motorcycle officers down Polk Street and across Market. They gave me a wave and turned left. I continued down Tenth Street and onto the James Lick Freeway. You want to know the easy way to find out if someone is following you? Without all the screeching of tires and bent fenders of Rockford, Starsky and Hutch, et al.? Just get on a freeway, speed up, then pull over to the side, like you're stopping to fix a flat. There's no place for the tail to go, except past you at fifty-five miles an hour. Unless he pulls over right behind you. Which was why I had the Magnum on my lap.

I crossed two lanes and skidded to a stop on the freeway's shoulder and watched the traffic flow by. Nobody who looked like Bill or José Cruz passed me, and nobody stopped behind me. I did it one more time just to be safe, then got off the freeway and dropped the Chevrolet off at the Hertz office on Mason Street and picked up the T-bird, which was parked in a red zone and had a ticket stuck under the windshield.

The first thing I wanted to do was stash the money somewhere safe. That meant Uncle Pee Wee.

"It is valuable to you, this case?" he asked.

"Very, uncle. There's a great deal of money inside the suitcase. And a letter addressed to the police. Inspector Bob Tehaney. If something happens to me, keep the money, but mail the envelope, please."

He chuckled. "Tehaney? He is still in the department? All right, Nicky. This sounds serious. Is there anything else I can do for you?"

"Yes, uncle." I handed him a small piece of paper. "Can you get this prescription filled?"

20

I headed south again, constantly checking the rearview mirror, stopped at the airport just long enough to rent a locker, then to a shopping mall where I loaded up on ammunition, then to a hardware store to pick up a hacksaw.

I spent a good two hours at the firing range at Coyote Point, running through the Magnum, the Spanish automatic, the Beretta and the little .25 I'd swiped from Kostas' apartment. I never was much of a shooter, but at least I now knew that all of the guns worked properly.

A Holiday Inn in South San Francisco was my next stop. I registered under the ever-popular name of Jim Smith and spent the afternoon cleaning the guns, sawing off the top half of the locker key, and keeping room service busy with drink orders. I had dinner alone in the motel dining room and was in bed with the television on by nine o'clock. Sleep seemed to come and go at about fifteen-minute intervals, and by six in the morning I was shaved, showered, and ready to go.

I drove by my flat four times before I felt confident that Bill wasn't camped nearby. The omnipresent Mrs. Damonte's blinds fluttered as I went up the stairs.

I checked out each room, Magnum in hand, feeling slightly foolish as I peeked behind doors and under the bed.

Now there was nothing to do but dress for the occasion and wait for the phone call.

The Magnum was big and bulky; the holster, with enough leather to make a saddle, stretched from under the shoulder to my waist. Nice and visible. Bill knew about the Beretta in the ankle holster, so it stayed right there. The Spanish automatic would have to go somewhere else. I fiddled around with it and finally settled on slipping it into the waistband at the back of my pants. There was an old TV show where the hero was always being checked for guns. The bad guys would frisk him all over, but never checked above the crack in his ass. He'd end up whipping out Old Faithful and shooting everybody full of holes until next week. Maybe Bald Bill hadn't seen the show, but I had a hunch he'd check there anyway. He knew about two guns, so he'd expect a third, but how about a fourth?

Being a lifelong coward when it came to having bandages pulled off, I shaved the area around the left side of my torso and used some plain white adhesive to tape Kostas' automatic to my skin. It took several tries to get it in the right spot, under the part where the Magnum's holster was the widest, but I finally got it positioned, barrel up, butt down, safety off, and bullet in the chamber. Now

159

if only I remembered not to scratch and blow a hole in my armpit, I just might be all right.

I wore a loose-fitting turtleneck sweater over the little gun, an old pair of gray slacks, tennis shoes, and a dark windbreaker. I hoped Bill wasn't picking any place fancy for the meeting. I'd hate to be underdressed.

I spent the next couple of hours drinking coffee, looking out onto the street, and trying to get comfortable with four guns hanging all over me. I felt like the National Rifle Association's Man of the Year.

Bill called right at ten o'clock. He left a brief, blunt message on the recorder. "Polo, be in Tiburon at Sam's Anchor Café in one hour. Or you're dead."

I left the flat, walked two blocks to where I'd left the T-bird, then went to see Uncle Pee Wee.

He greeted me warily. "Here is your prescription." He handed me a small white box. I opened it. All the capsules looked the same. He took a napkin from his pocket and unwrapped another capsule, identical to the ones in the box. "Here. The only one you'll have contact with, I trust." He grinned. "Olive oil, what else?"

Traffic was thin, so I had no problem in getting to Tiburon on time. Tiburon is a little gem of a town on the north side of the bay. The green Marin Hills surrounding it are dotted with expensive mansions, and there is a seaside promenade that caters to every whim of the tourists that flock there on weekends. The marinas are filled with everything from homemade skiffs to sleek schooners and power boats just under ocean liner size.

Sam's was filled with the boat-brunch crowd—lots of slick, brightly colored shirts and jackets over faded dungarees or white cords and Sperry Topsiders. A few show-offs in double-breasted blue blazers and captain's caps rubbed elbows at the bar with girls with perfect tans under striped tops and shorts. I ordered a gin fizz and waited. And waited. I nursed the fizz for a good twenty minutes, then switched to plain coffee, walking from the bar to the outside deck and back a good dozen times before a dark-haired guy in his twenties tapped me on the shoulder.

"You Polo?" he asked.

He was built low to the ground, and wide, like one of those fullbacks who was always called on when it was third down and inches to go from the goal line.

"That's me," I said.

"Guy told me to find you, give you a lift."

"A guy?"

"Said his name was Bill. Listen, you don't want to go, it's okay with me." He stretched and yawned, not bothering to cover his mouth. "I got paid already."

"Where are we going?"

He pointed a stubby finger out to the bay. "Over there. Angel Island."

I followed him through the restaurant, down to the dock, and into a small light blue, fiberglass inboard.

"What's your name, pal?" I said.

"Al," he answered indifferently as he cast off the lines, gunned the motor, and took off. There was a string of sailboats, like neatly folded handkerchiefs, between us and Angel Island. Al weaved through them expertly and in just a few minutes delivered me to the ferry terminal dock at Ayala Cove.

If you looked at a map of San Francisco Bay and Alcatraz was the size of a dime, Angel Island would be a silver dollar. There are a couple of old abandoned army forts, a coast guard station, hiking trails, and beaches. It's a popular spot for bike-riding, fishing, or just goofing off. The only way to reach it is by private boat or the ferry.

"Now what?" I asked, climbing onto the pier.

Al shrugged his sloping shoulders. "Don't know, man. He just paid me to drop you off here. Easiest fifty bucks I've made in a long time. Slong."

"Slong" for "so long." That was good. I'd have to remember to pass it on to Mrs. Damonte.

I lit one of Peckman's Cuban cigars to give my hands something to do rather than just shake. The sun had won its battle over the fog, and it was warm enough to go without a jacket. Except of course the tourists would take one look at my armaments and think the contras had invaded the island.

I lounged against a piling. One ferry boat came, discharging dozens of reasonably happy-looking adults and kids, loaded down with bicycles, fishing poles, backpacks, and picnic baskets.

I made two trips to the men's room, blaming it on lousy coffee rather than nervous kidneys, and just tried to look inconspicuous.

José Cruz was on the next ferry boat. I spotted him as soon as he got off. He walked right past me without giving me a glance. There was no sign of Bill. Cruz walked to the end of the pier and disappeared. I spotted him again a few minutes later. I squatted down Indian fashion and waited.

He came quickly, his crepe soles making a faint kissing sound on the damp planking.

"You got the money?" he said when he was no more than a few feet away.

Both my knees made popping sounds when I stood up. "Am I dealing with you, or Bill?"

His eyes darted nervously out to the water. "There's a rifle sighted in right between your shoulder blades. If you're not alone, or if you don't have the money, I'm going to make a signal and you're a dead man."

I flipped the cigar into the bay. "People keep threatening me with that, José. I'm ready to deal. What the hell, it's not my money anyway."

Cruz was just about even to me in height, but he was so lean, he looked taller. His jet black hair was still worn long, almost shoulder-length, and tied back with a red bandanna. Sunglasses the size of hubcaps covered his eyes. He stepped away from me, reached into his back pocket, pulled out a yellow scarf, and waved it over his head. My shoulders tightened involuntarily thinking about Bill out there watching all of this through a rifle scope.

Cruz put the scarf away and slid both hands into his jacket pockets. "No funny stuff, or I swear I'll shoot you right now. When the boat comes, just get in, nice and quiet."

He was bouncing up and down on the balls of his feet as he looked out at the bay. A nervous junkie with a gun in his jacket is the kind of guy I listen to. Very closely.

"Relax, José. I'll be a good boy."

163

The boat was a beautiful trawler and must have been close to fifty feet in length. It was all white. A royal blue swatch of canvas fastened down a small dinghy by the flying bridge. Whoever was handling it knew what he was doing. It caught the tide just right and came alongside the pier, water burbling softly against the sleek hull, the port side barely nudging the dock bumpers.

"In. Now!" Cruz shouted.

I jumped aboard. The aft deck was no more than six or eight feet. Cruz jumped down beside me and shoved me toward a door leading to the boat's stateroom. The stateroom was carpeted in a bright blue. The walls were paneled in rosewood and there was fishing gear hanging from the corked ceiling. Pictures of a heavyset man standing next to various-sized fish were sprinkled all over the place. A stuffed marlin sailed over a partition by a built-in bar. Cruz pulled a gun from his jacket pocket and ordered me to sit down. There were two couches covered in a cloth that matched the color of the rugs. Metal coffee tables painted to look like wood were bolted to the floor in front of the couches. I sat obediently. "How about a beer, José?"

"Fuck you, man. I ain't your servant."

"You want a beer, Polo?"

I swiveled my neck so fast I almost fell off the couch. Holding a beer in his hand was Walter Peckman. He was wearing the same blue suit, white shirt, and striped tie that he had on yesterday in his office. The shirt collar was open and soiled; the tie was at half-mast. He walked uncertainly and handed me a can of beer.

"Surprised?" he said.

"Yeah. You could say that. Where's Talbot? Down below cleaning fish? This is turning into quite a party."

"José, take the wheel."

I pulled my eyes from Peckman and looked at Bill. He was all in white: pants, shirt, shoes, even the knit cap on his head. A rifle that looked like another ugly reminder of Vietnam, an AR-16 with an extralong clip, was hanging casually from his right hand.

"Well, Lucky. We meet again." His eyes turned hard, and he moved the barrel of the rifle up so that it was no more than six inches from my chest.

"I don't see the money," he said.

"I didn't bring it. But I've got the key to the locker that it's in."

"Stand up," he ordered, prodding the rifle barrel into my stomach, then under my jacket.

"Peckman, get over here. Get his gun."

Peckman's hands were trembling when he pulled the Magnum from its holster. He handed it to Bill, who tucked it in his waistband.

"Check his pants leg. See if he brought his little Beretta with him."

Peckman dutifully bent down and pulled out the Beretta. Bill snatched it from his hand, then opened the door leading aft and threw it overboard.

"Now, Lucky, I know you. You like to be cute. So somewhere there's another gun, right?" He jammed the rifle barrel into my chest and with one hand patted down both my legs. "Turn around. Slowly."

I turned around. Very slowly.

"What did you think you were going to do with

165

this?" he asked when he found the Spanish automatic at the base of my spine. "I'm beginning to think you don't trust me."

He reversed the rifle and smashed the butt end into the back of my knee.

I sank to the carpeted deck in pain. Between clenched teeth I said, "Don't do that again. Not if you want to see the money."

"No? How you going to stop me?" He aimed the rifle at my face. "How?"

"My right-hand pants pocket has a box in it. Take a look."

"Get it," he told Peckman.

Peckman's hands felt cold as they reached into my trousers. His face was starting to show a little green under its normal beet red.

"Here," he said, thrusting the little white box at Bill.

He took it, read the typed pharmacy label that said the contents were sodium cyanide, then opened it. His face showed no emotion. "What the fuck am I supposed to do with these? Commit suicide?"

I rose to my feet in a commendable attempt at looking confident. "No, but I will." I smiled, opened my mouth, and showed him the capsule between my teeth. "I'm not into pain, Bill. You try roughing me up, playing the happy little torturer, and I'll end it right now. I know what my chances are of leaving this boat alive anyway, so you push it and so help me you'll end up with nothing. I've got an envelope in my inside jacket pocket. You better take a look at that too."

He shook his head angrily. "I knew you'd try something cute. I was expecting a stick of dynamite up your ass, or something more dramatic than a bunch of phony pills."

"If you think they're phony, try one."

He brought the rifle barrel up again. "Let's see what you got in your jacket."

I handed him the envelope. He backed away, sat down, laying the rifle across his lap, opened the envelope, and laughed when he saw the drawings of Cruz and himself.

"Nice work. You do these yourself?"

"I had help."

"Hey, José. Come out here. Take a look at this."

There was a partition that blocked most of the wheelhouse from view. An opening to the right of the wheelhouse appeared to be a stairway leading down below-decks. The engine idled down to almost a full stop and the boat started drifting. Cruz stomped out to join us, snatched the drawing away from Bill, took one look at it, and crumpled it up and threw it at me. His only comment was "Asshole."

"This is real impressive shit," Bill said. "But I still want to know where the money is."

I held my palms up. "Okay if I reach into my pocket?"

"Sure, just do it real slow."

I took out the cutoff key. "The money's in a suitcase, in the locker this key fits." I dropped the key onto the carpet and kicked it over to him.

When he bent over to pick it up, I folded my arms,

my right hand creeping under the Magnum's holster, my fingers touching the butt of the small automatic through my sweater. It felt awfully reassuring.

"Cute, cute, cute," Bill said as he studied the key. "Now what am I supposed to do to get you to tell me just where this locker is."

"Give me all the Barbara Martin material. Pictures, negatives, tapes, all of it."

"Shit," he snorted. "You risked your balls for that crap. It's worthless now."

"I'd like to see it anyway."

He nodded and handed Cruz the rifle. "Watch this sneaky bastard real close, José," he said, then went down the steps leading belowdecks.

I eased my way back onto the couch. "Tell me, Peckman," I said, massaging the back of my knee. "What's your part in all this now? When did you join up with this outfit?"

"I made a deal with him when he called me that day about the money. Hell, I wasn't going to pay them anything for that junk they had on Barbara. They'd never use it with her dead. He was just bluffing. And I called his bluff." He burped and patted his ample stomach. "But this is a resourceful fellow, Polo. Barbara wasn't his only target. He has the goods on quite a few people: the present lieutenant governor, some assemblymen, and old squeaky-clean Lawrence Talbot himself. Nothing like that garbage with Barbara, but good solid dirt—kickbacks, that kind of thing."

"Then why the big charade? Why use me to run your errands?"

"For Talbot's sake, of course. The big law-and-order man is up in Seattle now, probably hiding under the bed with his wife. And believe me, if you ever met his wife, you wouldn't want to get into cramped quarters with her. No wonder the poor bastard was fooling around with Barbara."

"Talbot? He was the one Martin was meeting?"

"Yes. I thought it was Kostas, but it was Talbot. I never figured he had the balls."

I studied Peckman. His face was flushed from the booze, his voice was a little slurred, but he was sitting there, like a white Buddha, content, patting his stomach, as emotional as if he were discussing the weather, or the 49er's point spread.

"Doesn't it bother you that your new partner set up Martin, did all those things to her, drove her to her death. Doesn't that bother you at all, Peckman?"

He pulled a face as if he had suddenly bitten into a sour lemon. "Barbara took her own life, damn it. It was all so unnecessary. And anyway, it was Kostas' idea to take the pictures. He sandbagged Talbot when he was getting ready to drive down to St. Helena. It was all Kostas' plan. Talbot didn't know a thing. *This* man was just carrying out orders." He waved a hand vaguely. "Things got out of hand up there, no doubt about it. I didn't like it. I told him so."

"You told him so? I bet that scared the shit out of him, didn't it?"

Peckman leaned back in the couch with the air of a man who was through for the day. "You just don't understand, do you? What's past is past. It's now you've always got to worry about. Clout, that's the only thing that counts, Polo. Clout. With enough clout, anything's possible."

"Clout, huh? Kostas had clout. Where's he at now?"

"You boys having a nice chat?" Bill asked, coming topside with a cardboard case that formerly held bottles of Cutty Sark Scotch. The box made a thud when he dropped it to the floor. "Don't worry about Kostas. He'll pop up one of these days."

"When the ropes holding him to the cement blocks give way?" I said.

"It's all in there, Polo. All of it. Take a look."

There were three videocassettes and a dozen or more plain white envelopes stuffed with pictures and negatives.

"Take a good look. You'll like the ones with Satan."

"I've seen enough."

"Good, now tell me about this little key."

"It's to a locker at San Francisco International Airport."

"Which one?" This from Cruz.

"Don't even think about just going to the airport and trying all the lockers. There are hundreds, and the cops would get suspicious as hell watching you try them all."

"The number, asshole," Cruz said, coming at me.

"We go down there together. I'll show it to you. You get the money and I walk away. It's that simple."

"Bullshit!" Cruz roared.

"I don't like it," Bill said. "I don't like it at all. I think I'm just going to start shooting you, in the arms, legs, places like that, until you tell me the locker number."

"The first shot you take, I'm swallowing the pill."

"He's bluffing," Cruz said. "Shoot him."

"Call the bluff, José. You try one of the pills."

Bill said, "What's your opinion, Peckman? Is he bluffing?"

Peckman sighed, wiped his face, and nodded, all at the same time. "Yes, I think he is."

Bill smiled at him. "Me too, but just to be sure, you're going to try one first."

Peckman made the mistake of opening his mouth to protest, and Bill was on him like a cat. Peckman's arms flapped wildly as a pill was forced down his mouth. He struggled to get up from the couch, but he was no match for the stronger, younger man. His face went gray, and his hands started pulling frantically at the loose skin around his neck. He cried out something that sounded like "Jesus help me," but I couldn't be sure. He flopped around on the couch for a few seconds, then was suddenly very still.

"Holy shit," Cruz said. "What the hell kind of junk was that?"

"Sodium cyanide. They called them mydies in 'Nam, don't you remember, José? Or maybe you never saw them. But I bet you did, eh, Bill. The spooks, and guys like you in Special Services, carried them in case they got caught by Charlie. The Cong had some dandy ways of killing people, didn't they? I remember a young kid from Oklahoma in our unit. That was all he ever talked about. Being captured alive and tortured. He bought some of the damn pills from a CIA spook. Not pretty, but quick."

"You could still be bluffing, Polo. Maybe that's nothing but a vitamin pill in your mouth."

"Maybe. But why risk testing me? I've got the money. You can have it. All I want to do is get out of this in one piece."

He grunted, then handed the rifle to Cruz and went up to the wheelhouse. We were out by the Golden Gate Bridge now. The engines returned to full power, and we went under the bridge, the Marin coast looming to our right. The fog had rolled in and there were only a few small fishing boats and a huge lumbering oil tanker in sight, and they were a good two miles away. We stayed on a western heading until we were past Point Bonita, then the boat turned north.

Bill came out, went down below again, and came back with a machete; the gleaming blade looked to be at least three feet long. He dragged Peckman out to the aft deck, raised the machete over his shoulder, brought it down with a thud, and severed Walter Peckman's head from his body. There were two more quick, vicious swipes with the machete, and Peckman's arms were cut off.

Cruz made a retching sound.

"What's the matter, José?" Bill yelled. "A little blood never used to bother you." He picked up Peckman's head by the hair and casually tossed it overboard. "How about the watch, José? You want it?"

Cruz's answer was more vomiting.

Bill looked at me with wild eyes. "You can't trust a gook, can you, Lucky?" He pulled Peckman's Rolex from the bloody stump that used to be a part of a human being, then threw both arms over the side, wiping his own bloody hands down the sides of his white pants.

"José, shape up. Keep an eye on Lucky here. We're going up the coast a ways to feed the sharks what's left of that pompous asshole, then we're all going to take a ride down to the airport." He swung the machete back and forth in front of him slowly. "And that locker better be there, and the money better be there, Polo, or I'm gonna chop you up so small, we'll have to feed you to goldfish."

I watched him disappear into the wheelhouse.

The boat's motors revved up as it was taken out of autopilot. We started a lazy turn to starboard, heading up north toward Bolinas. The waves were coming in from the sandbars of Potato Patch Shoals, and as we bobbed up and down, Peckman's torso started rolling back and forth on the aft deck.

Cruz was starting to feel sick again, and as he leaned over the sink by the wet bar, I reached under my sweater. He saw me out of the corner of his eye and swiveled the rifle at me.

"What the fuck are you—"

I fell to my knees and gasped. "The pill, damn it, I swallowed . . ." I went down on all fours, my back to Cruz, my hand going under the turtleneck, pulling the little gun free.

Cruz came toward me cautiously, and I straightened up and fired when he was no more than three feet away. Three quick shots, right at his chest. He screamed, the rifle clattered to the floor, and he fell on top of me. I struggled free just in time to see Bill running from the wheelhouse. He took one look at me, spun on his heel, and dove down the steps leading below deck. I snapped off two quick shots that crashed harmlessly into a wall.

I pushed Cruz away and grabbed the rifle. I was right. It was an AR-16. I aimed toward the front of the boat and pulled the trigger. A burst of shots went off before I could remove my finger. At least I didn't have to worry about the safety being on.

The boat was running free now, one time heading into the waves, the next moment being hit broadside.

I got to my knees and pushed Cruz's body ahead of me, using it as a shield, the rifle laying across his shoulders. It was tough pushing. A good-sized wave hit us head-on, shoving the bow up, and Cruz and I slid back down toward the stern.

So far, Bill hadn't shown himself. I wondered what kind of armament he had with him down below.

The wind started to howl as the boat was buffeted helplessly back and forth. I started shoving Cruz's body forward again. We went down into a deep swell, and I could see the white, jagged shoreline to my right. We were being pushed right into the rocks. I maneuvered close to the stairwell, timed a wave just right and heaved Cruz's body down the stairs. There was a thunderous burst of shots, then silence. We were even now. Just Bill and me. He had a gun. Probably my Magnum from the sound of it. Even. Then why did I feel like the odds of my surviving were about five to one against. Bill was a professional, I wasn't. It was that simple. So I'd have to get lucky. Again.

I looked around for some help. There were two red fire extinguishers strapped to the wall. I took them down one at a time. Quietly. The rocks were getting closer now. I knew just how cold the water could be and that there was little chance of surviving the hypothermia, even if I somehow got by the jagged rocks, the pounding surf, and the undertow.

I put one of the extinguishers between my legs, the other under my left arm, and crawled back to the stair-well.

"We're heading for the rocks, Billy Boy. In another couple of minutes we'll be nothing but splinters. Why don't you come up? We'll call a truce. You can still have the money."

Silence. Bill was saving his bullets. Or was he just waiting for me to panic? There was no porthole below, so he had no way of knowing if we were drifting into shore or not.

"I'm not waiting to die on those rocks," I yelled against the roaring wind. "One of us is going to have to take the wheel, or we're both going to die."

Still no response. Bill's mama didn't raise no stupid boy. Though she certainly raised a mean one.

The rocks were getting closer. Another few minutes and we'd be in them. Or under them.

I nudged the extinguishers close to the stairs, then threw them both down and, while they were tumbling, opened fire.

I counted to five, then dove down the steps. My eyes burned and my lungs soon filled up with the chalky air. I couldn't see anything but a blur of white powder. I started spraying shots around the cabin, left, right, up and down, then ran back up the steps, falling on the deck, coughing uncontrollably.

When my eyes cleared, I saw we were no more than a hundred yards from the jagged shoreline. Gray water was crashing wildly against the rocks.

The wheel was spinning out of control. I grabbed it, pushing and turning as hard as I could. The boat reacted sluggishly, moaning and groaning as if it were alive, fighting for its life, like I was. We moved inch by inch to port and toward the open sea. We'd make a little headway, then another big wave would catch us sideways and shove us closer to the shoreline.

I kept working the wheel. The boat's control panel was a maze of brass and teak levers, plastic buttons, and dials. I wanted to increase power, but if I pushed the wrong button, or pulled the wrong lever, the motors might die, and then there'd be nothing left to do but jump overboard and pray for a miracle.

I don't know how long it took, minutes or hours, but I finally got the bow straightened out and away from the rocks.

"Nice going."

I spun around and looked down at Bill's grinning face. His whole body seemed to be a mixture of the CO_2 powder from the extinguishers and blood. He was lying down, both his hands holding my Magnum. The thumb of his right hand moved and there was a click as the hammer snapped into the firing position.

"Game's over, Lucky."

"Not yet. Don't forget about the key. You want the money, why don't you—"

A massive wave hit and sent the boat reeling, plunging into the angry swells. The Magnum went off, the shot coming so close I could feel the breeze as it passed. I kicked out at Bill's hands as he struggled to get to his feet. The gun skidded down the carpet. He straightened up, still grinning, his eyes wild, teeth bared like an animal. A big, dangerous animal that liked killing. From the amount of blood on his shirt, I knew that he was wounded, but he moved easily, his hands out and open, waving me in.

"Come on, Lucky. Come and get me."

The boat was bobbing up and down like a yo-yo again. I waited for the next roll, then dove at him. He brought a leg up toward my groin, but the boat's motion threw him off balance. I got in close, where I wanted to be, and landed an elbow hard in his chest. He grunted, countered my next punch, and brought the heel of his hand down across my neck, missing the vital spot but still sending dizzy shock waves all the way down my spine. I twisted my legs around his and pulled him to the ground. We rolled around, grabbing at each other, and even though he was hurt, I had no doubt he was the stronger man.

He could feel it too, as his slippery hands worked their way up around my neck. I kept swinging with knees and elbows, but they seemed to have little effect. I could feel myself starting to go, the power leaving my arms. He just kept grinning, the fire in his eyes getting brighter. I got an arm up by his face, grabbed his hair, and pulled his head down to me, opening my mouth and biting down hard enough on his nose to draw blood. He cried out, his head twisted madly, but I held on like a terrier, my hands moving now, digging for his eyes. I found the sockets and pushed in. His hands left my neck, and I kicked out and scrambled free, crawling down the floor. The Magnum had ended up under one of the tables. I grabbed the gun and turned to see Bill, swaying back and forth, his bloodied hands massaging his eyes.

He sank to his knees and sat on the floor.

"Lucky," he roared. "Where are you?"

"Right here. I've got the gun. So don't move."

"So you won, huh? Now what?" He pulled his hands from his eyes and blinked rapidly, his head shaking. "Ah, there you are. Now what?"

"Now I'm going to kill you, Bill."

He was taking deep breaths, his eyes on the gun, getting ready to make one final attack.

"You and I got something, Lucky, you know that? We were in 'Nam together. What outfit were you in?"

"The 101st."

"Hey, I know a lot of guys from that outfit. You guys were okay. Damn good, in fact. We're brothers. War brothers. You know how it was over there." He waved an arm out. "These other assholes don't. Got back and they treated us like pieces of shit." He was on his knees now, hands on his hips, his brain probably calculating the distance between us, figuring that I might get in one shot and one shot only.

"Tell you what, Lucky. You give me half of the money and I'll go somewhere and you'll never hear from me again, what do you say?"

He was leaning forward. I could see the toes of his shoes wiggling into the carpet.

"I've got just the place for you, Bill. Go to hell."

The gun went off just as he started his leap.

21

"Can I get you a drink, sir?"

The waiter was wearing white shorts and a green and yellow shirt with trees and flowers on it.

"Yes, a couple of daiquiris."

"What kind, sir? Banana? Strawberry? Peach? Pineapple?"

I took off my sunglasses and looked up at him. He was a nice-looking kid in his mid-twenties, dark haired, clear-skinned. Could be a native. "Just the old-fashioned plain kind, son."

He wrote down the order on a cocktail napkin and plodded off in the sand. I looked over the beach and sighed. It was a gorgeous day. The kind of day you pay for and expect in Hawaii. Waikiki Beach was filled with sun lovers of every age and size. The girls in skimpy bikinis that couldn't be worn without the aid of an electrologist were getting both admiring and disgusted glances as they pranced by, depending on who was doing the looking.

"Are you through with the sports page?" Jill Ashbury asked.

I nodded, folded up the Sports section, and reached over and handed it to her. She passed me the *San Francisco Chronicle*'s front-page section.

Jill was hugging the shade, allowing her fair skin, which was smothered in a sweet-smelling sun lotion, only an hour of sun a day. She was wearing a beautiful emerald green suit that looked almost Victorian compared to what the competition was basking in.

The mainland papers were a day late; still, they made interesting reading. Page 3 had a story on the strange yacht found anchored in Richardson Bay. Passing boats had noticed numerous bullet holes in the vessel and had reported it to the police. There was no one on board. The boat had been traced to its owner, a Mr. Roy Zerbe of Stockton, who had reported it stolen over a week ago.

Police theorized that the boat could have been involved in a narcotics operation and may be tied to the unidentified body of a man washed ashore on the Marin coastline. The body, that of a heavily muscled white male adult in his mid-thirties, had been shot prior to being in the water, the coroner's office stated. Anyone with any information was asked to contact the Marin County Sheriff's Office.

The waiter placed the daiquiris on a short-legged metal tray. "Do you want to sign for these, sir?"

I handed him a fifty. "No, son. Cash. I like to pay cash for everything."

ST. MARTIN'S PRESS
The First Name in Great Mysteries

THE JOHN CREASEY CRIME COLLECTION,
volume 1
Herbert Harris, editor

Murder, mystery and mayhem—British style. Fifteen stories by modern masters: P.D. James, Peter Lovesey, Julian Symons, Michael Gilbert, H.R.F. Keating and others.

_____90128-3 $3.50 U.S.

MURDER AT BUCKINGHAM PALACE
T.E.B. Clarke

Upstairs, royalty was preparing for the 1935 Royal Jubilee...downstairs, a pretty housemaid was being murdered. "A marvelous novel of privilege and murder most foul."—*Denver Post*

_____90286-7 $2.95 U.S.

SHERLOCK HOLMES AND THE CASE
OF THE RALEIGH LEGACY
L.B. Greenwood

Only the master himself could decipher the letter that was the Raleigh legacy. "The game is afoot again, and a glorious game it is, too.... If Holmes didn't already have legions of fans, this book would create them." —*Philadelphia Daily News*

_____90843-1 $2.95 U.S.   _____90845-8 $3.95 Can.

THE RED DIAMOND MYSTERIES
by Mark Schorr

When cabbie Simon Jaffe's wife hocks his treasured collection of thirties pulp magazines, it sends Simon over the edge—and onto the streets with a new identity: Red Diamond, Private Eye

RED DIAMOND, PRIVATE EYE
"A tour de force..."   —Newgate Callendar,
                                    The New York Times Book Review
_____90657-9 $3.95 U.S.   _____90658-7 $4.95 Can.

ACE OF DIAMONDS
Simon Jaffe, aka Red Diamond, takes on the big boys in Las Vegas for a high stakes game of murder and revenge.
_____90663-3 $3.95 U.S.   _____90664-1 $4.95 Can.

DIAMOND ROCK
Red's quest for a mob boss named Becker sends him straight to L.A., where Red is faced with a deadly world of soft porn, hard drugs, and heavy metal—heavy like lead that's got his name on it.
_____90661-7 $3.95 U.S.   _____90662-5 $4.95 Can.